THE DARK SIDE OF THE ROOM

TYLER JONES

DARK ROOM PRESS

Copyright © Tyler Jones, 2021

Cover design by Tyler Jones

Interior title illustrations by Ryan Mills
rtm.art.inq@gmail.com

Interior layout by Scott Cole
www.13visions.com

All rights reserved

This book is a work of fiction. Names, characters, places, and incidents are either products of the author's imagination or are used fictitiously. Any resemblance to actual events, locales, or persons, living or dead, is entirely coincidental.
No part of this publication may be reproduced or transmitted in any form or by any means, electronic or mechanical, without written permission from the author.

For more information about the author, visit
www.tylerjones.net

INTRODUCTION

Discovery.

What a great word, right? What an inspiring concept.

Discovery—*real* discovery—can often be transcendent. For many, the feeling can be borderline religious. The rush of something new. Something exceptional.

A new planet! A new species!

Pirate ship ruins—packed with treasure—found within the dark depths of an ocean canyon.

A great song you'd never heard.

A fantastic author you'd never read.

For me? There's nothing more thrilling than the

discovery of a writer. Someone who may not be new to the scene, per se, but is still new to me.

It's a rush, man. Opening a book and fixing on that first page, nodding along, digging it, grooving on it. And then, losing myself in it. Carried away by the prose, by the story, by the rhythm of the writing. Feeling that *connection.*

The first time I read Tyler Jones it hit me like that. On all cylinders.

Honestly, when I first picked up *The Dark Side of the Room,* my expectations were fairly low. Not because I didn't believe I'd enjoy the story (I'd heard nothing but rave reviews from other readers I follow on social media), but because I read a lot. And by that I mean:

I read a LOT.

So for me to pick up something unfamiliar and immediately lose myself, get that sensation of discovery that I've been talking about—to feel like I was reading something fresh, something I connected with so easily—was, as The Dude likes to say: *Far out, man*!

Far out, yeah, but even better? Completely unexpected.

But it just goes to show you that sometimes the

indie scene can surprise you. It can catch you off guard. It can reveal new voices—exciting, original voices—that you might have otherwise missed when picking up that umpteenth thriller from the Walmart rack, or the newest YA fantasy getting all that ink over at *Entertainment Weekly*.

And while I can't describe Tyler's writing to you (and there's really no need, because in a few hundred words you're gonna be getting a taste of it for yourself), I can tell you what impressed me so much about his storytelling, and what propelled me to read *The Dark Side of the Room* cover-to-cover in a single sitting (okay, minus a fridge run for a Diet Coke). Which, by the way, is another rare achievement, because while I'm an avid reader, or as Uncle Steve likes to say, a *constant* reader, I'm also an insanely, compulsively, finicky reader. I'm usually digging through four or five different books over a period of a few hours, switching from one to the other, my attention nagging at me to jump between stories like I'm turning television stations. So for me to get locked into a book, even a novella-length one, and burn through from beginning to end? Man, that's rare as a peacock stumbling into your living room, full plume (and just as delightful).

That all said, what captivated me about the story you're about to read was partly the prose, partly the way Tyler kept surprising me with new information, partly the underlying, expansive themes I could sense percolating beneath the text, and partly the speed with which the author moved the story along (I'd suggest getting that Diet Coke after this introduction and before you start the main attraction). But primarily, in retrospect, I think what carried me like a perfect wave through this dark, tragic, horror-fueled novella, was the humanity of it all. I *cared* about these characters, about Betsy, in particular. I felt her fear. Her despair. Her *loss*. It affected my mind and my heart in a way only a great story can.

Because, ultimately, that's one of the biggest reasons we read books in the first place. To be entertained, yeah, of course. But to be *moved?* Man, that's what brings the booze to the party. That's the juice that hits your veins and makes your fingers spark like exposed cables, eager to flip the pages; makes your jaw clench and your eyes narrow in worry, in fear, in anxious sorrow, while your eyes dance and dance down the words.

But the last thing I want to tell you about *The Dark Side of the Room*, and about the way Tyler tells this story, goes beyond the thrill of discovery, the swirling elation of empathy. What struck me the hardest was the delicate beauty of the telling. There's a tight-wired fragility to the prose, to the story, that creates a sense of both awe and uncertainty. Imagine a crystal glass filled with ink-black liquid. Don't drop it! And for God's sakes, don't drink it!

Or hey, you know what?

Do it.

Hell yeah, slug the dark potion back and down that hatch, then hurl that haunted cut-glass goblet into the fireplace, because that's what Tyler wants. It's what the story desires. To shatter you. To crawl inside your veins and give your head and heart a couple little twists.

To exhilarate you. To frighten you.

It's all here, waiting for you to turn the page.

To discover something new.

Philip Fracassi
February, 2021

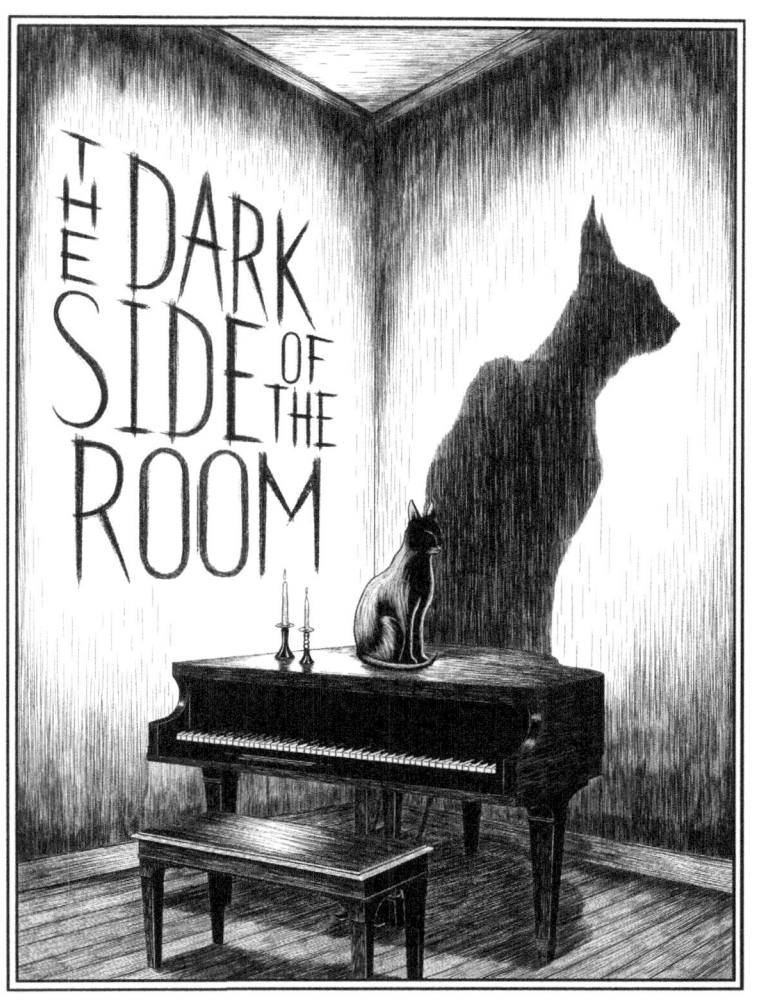

PART I

MINOR KEYS

From *The Oregonian*

Another body was found near a homeless encampment in the Pearl District last night, marking the sixth victim of a killer who appears to be targeting the city's indigent population. As with the previous five cases, the corpse was decapitated. The heads have not been recovered.

1

Betsy Lupino saw the new resident before the others, and the first thing she noticed was how funny the man walked. Like he was disabled or something. Injured, maybe. He came stumbling into the Parkrose apartments from the storm outside, rain water dripping off his clothes into a puddle on the carpet of the lobby. Carpet so stained no one but Betsy remembered its original color. She'd been living here since Robert died, and that was so long ago she couldn't even think of the year.

The man took one step with his right leg and sort of dragged the left behind it. The toes of his shoe scuffed along the carpet. He was bent backwards, but with each step his upper body would fling forward, as if on a hinge, and his arms flailed to right himself. The head bobbed back and forth like one those little toys Betsy's granddaughter used to like.

The clothes he wore were all black, and baggy, like the man had recently dropped a lot of weight and his frame was lost in all the fabric. His long, black overcoat was covered in mud and water, and underneath he wore a sweatshirt with the hood pulled up over his head. The hood was so big it kept most of his face in shadow, but Betsy saw the scratches. Dozens of them. Short and deep all over his chin and nose. Red open sores covered his cheeks, what she could see of them. His eyes were hidden somewhere in the hood, too far back for her to see, but Betsy thought she saw a little light reflecting off his pupils.

The man came into the lobby like a drunk on a ship at sea, and stopped when he saw Betsy, who had just come home from the store and was still holding a reusable grocery bag filled with cans of cat food and a new bottle of linseed oil for her piano.

She set down the bag and folded up her umbrella, watching as the man swayed back and forth. The coat was so long that the sleeves completely covered his hands, so he looked like an amputee. Betsy didn't own a cell phone, but depending on what this man did next, she was ready to run to Al's apartment and ask him to call the cops. Although the superintendent was mostly worthless, she knew how much he hated druggies wandering into his building and stealing the mail, trying door handles to see if any were unlocked.

If he was disabled, Betsy certainly didn't want to stare, but she could also feel the man staring at her, as if challenging her to acknowledge him. He could at least take care of himself, though, or hire someone to help him. Weren't there programs for people like him? Betsy always felt uncomfortable around people who were obviously disabled, and she couldn't stop it. Physical deformities of any kind made her stomach flutter like when she saw a huge python in a nature documentary. Made her skin crawl a bit. She didn't like that she felt that way, it was just her wiring.

The man's head leaned forward a little and she saw the cracked lips, scabbed over sores around the half open mouth. And God, the smell. Like rotten meat and something else…something she couldn't quite place.

Water dripped from a dark stain on the ceiling and fell to the floor between them. Betsy looked up, the man did not.

Betsy nodded at the leak. "Only does that when it's been raining over six hours straight. Otherwise, God knows where the water goes. Probably turning to mold in the walls."

Betsy wagged one finger and squinted. "Do you even live here?"

Something Betsy could only think of as a "ripple" moved up the strange man's body. A shiver that started at his feet (old leather shoes split along the sole and showing dirty white socks) and rolled up his legs, into his hips and chest, and all the way to his neck. It reminded her of wind moving through a sail.

The man righted himself and stood as straight as it seemed he could, which was still crooked. Painful looking, Betsy thought. A spine injury, perhaps? The man tilted his head toward the ceiling. She saw the glow of his eyes again, small pinpoints in the dark of the hood.

Betsy said. "Upstairs? Are you new tenant taking Campbell's old place?"

The man nodded again, and the motion caused a whiff of his odor to drift over and Betsy faked a yawn to cover to her gag. So rotten. And not like what she would expect from a person. This was the smell of a dumpster behind a restaurant, full of food scraps, turned dairy, and dead animals. What she didn't smell, though, was alcohol. And that pleased her. She didn't like people who drank. Didn't trust them. Whether trying to drown pain or become stupid, it was no way to live and she didn't approve of it.

Betsy picked up her grocery bag and gave the new resident a tight smile.

"Best be getting my cat her dinner," she said.

The man's hooded head fell forward, then came back up in a slow nod.

He hasn't said a word, Betsy thought. *Must be a mute.*

Campbell's old place was just down the hall from Betsy's apartment on the fourth floor, and she felt a little guilty that she did not want this man anywhere near her. Not on her floor, not in her building. Seemed that Al would rent to anyone these days.

Betsy made her way to the stairs and started up. She had to hold the railing like an old woman, which she supposed she was, because her neuropathy made her feet go so numb she could barely feel them sometimes. And a tumble down the stairs was something she did *not* need.

She turned to see the man standing at the elevator,

head tilted off to one side like he was listening.

"Hey," Betsy called down.

The man's head straightened, and then fell to the other side. He moved his body in an awkward shuffle so that he half faced her.

"The elevator don't work," Betsy said. "Gotta take the stairs."

The man's head lolled back to the center, then backward, like he was looking up at the ceiling. And he stood there, saying nothing.

The bag of cat food got heavier with each step, and Betsy swore yet again that she'd try harder to get rid of the extra twenty pounds she couldn't seem to lose. She kept expecting to hear the man's footsteps climbing up behind her—he'd probably pass her, the way she walked—but there was only her squeaky shoes and heavy breathing. By the time she made it up to the fourth floor, Betsy Lupino was winded and sweating. The grocery bag had creased a red line in the palm of her hand and it hurt. She wanted to call Jerry, tell him about their new neighbor and how strange he was. Especially how bad he smelled. She knew Jerry would find that repulsive.

She had told the new resident that she had to feed

her cat, but the mewling coming from the other side of the door as she slipped her key into the deadbolt was not just from one cat, it was from several. A brown one lounged on the rug in the blue glow of the TV. A grey one slunk along the back of the couch, staring at the bag in Betsy's hand. Another slept on one of the three scratching posts lined up against the wall. Two more lay on top of the baby grand piano in the corner.

Betsy had never told anyone just how many cats she had, and if pressed on the matter she'd say two, because that seemed like a reasonable number. Not too crazy. But the fact was, Betsy Lupino shared her apartment with five cats, with a sixth who came and went out the living room window as he pleased.

Time passed, the rain fell, and Betsy stood in a trance. She was about to do something, but now she couldn't think of what it was. She hated it when this happened. It made her feel so old and frail. She'd gone to the grocery store, met the new resident, come back home, and…what the D-sharp was it?

Betsy thought of her head as a room, and all of the furniture and objects inside it represented memories, moments lived, lessons learned. Part of that room was always in the dark, and she had the terrible feeling that important things were hidden there. Things she could no longer see or reach. And even worse, she feared that the dark side of the room was growing bigger by the day, overtaking things she had once been able to see so clearly. Advancing through the comfort of her safe space, day by day, inch by inch. It wouldn't be long before all of it was dark and she could no longer find her way through the room.

Pleading meows pulled her out of the Memory Room, and she looked down at the heavy bags full of cat food she still gripped in each hand. Several cats had gathered around her feet, weaving between her ankles and nudging the bags.

"Goodness," Betsy said. "Of course, you all must be starving."

Betsy opened up some cans and dumped the food into the five bowls in the kitchen. She couldn't stop thinking about the man in the lobby, about the weird way his body moved. There was something else, though. Something she hadn't been able to think of until the cats began slinking into the kitchen. She silently counted them as they rubbed against her legs on their way to the bowls.

THE DARK SIDE OF THE ROOM

Betsy felt eyes staring at her, looked up, and saw Starry sitting on the counter, looking right at her. Starry because he was black with white spots. The cat stared without expression or emotion, and that's when Betsy realized what had been bothering her. The man in the lobby, the whole time she talked to him he hadn't blinked once.

2

Thunder boomed and shook the windows, followed a few seconds later by a flash of light, and then the power went out. The TV turned off and the room was plunged into darkness. Betsy kept the TV going day and night for the cats, and the sudden quiet was startling. She heard her own breathing, which was far more wheeze than breath due to the climb up the stairs.

Al was supposed to get the elevator fixed two months ago. She had no evidence that the man was a pervert, but Betsy always imagined him in his first-floor apartment with something unsavory playing in the background. Not that she could blame him. Al was a disgusting man, overweight with a balding head and a body odor problem. The few strands of hair he did have were constantly slick with sweat and pasted to his forehead. He couldn't find a woman (or a man, depending on his preference) even if he took a shower and smiled—his teeth were the brownish yellow of Dijon mustard.

Betsy opened the junk drawer and rummaged until she found the flashlight. She turned it on and shone it around the living room. Bright eyes glowed from the couch, the floor, underneath the TV stand. Another pair of eyes darted down the hall to the bedroom.

"Alright," Betsy said out loud. "Settle down."

From the drawer she took out some half-burned candles and a cigarette lighter. She lit the candles, dripped some wax into the bottom of several coffee cups and stuck the candles inside. She put one on the dining room table, one by the TV, and two more on the kitchen counter. The soft flicker bathed the apartment in an orange glow.

More thunder cracked and some of the cats scrambled for hiding places. Betsy hoped they wouldn't leave a mess someplace she couldn't find it. That happened once before and she had to spray Lysol everywhere to cover up the smell until she found it, in one of her potted plants.

The room went bright as lightning flashed, closer

this time, and she saw the silhouette of Shadow, her sixth cat, the gray one, just outside on the fire escape. His head was turned, looking out at the city and all the darkened buildings. The storm did not seem to bother him.

She moved the flashlight beam around, unsure what to do. The circle of light landed on a framed photograph hung on the wall. A picture of Betsy and her daughter Kristy, pregnant at the time with Jules. Kristy's hand rested on her round belly, and her smile was big and genuine, eyes squinting in the sun that shone on her. A cheap necklace hung off one corner of the frame—a Mother's Day gift that Betsy wore for years even though the chain turned her skin green.

How many years had it been, Betsy wondered? And what did Jules look like now, the child growing inside that stomach-bump? Betsy thought back to the falling out, when Kristy called and said she was no longer welcome at their home. Said she couldn't deal with her mother's "mental health issues" any longer. Betsy had laughed at the time. What issues? She didn't drink, or smoke, or gamble, or take any pills to numb whatever inner pain she might have. She took care of her cats, knitted hats and booties for infants in the NICU at the nearby hospital, and did crossword puzzles when she had trouble sleeping. Her "mental health issues," such as they were, cast almost no shadow over her life. But Kristy put her foot down, said Dan agreed with her, and as far Jules would be concerned, she would have no grandmother.

The photograph, better times. *Maybe the whole world was better then*, Betsy thought. She moved the flashlight beam and the picture went back into darkness. She felt loneliness creep up inside her chest, like a cat stealing into her room at night.

She went to the front door, unlocked it, took a quick look at her cats and prayed they wouldn't knock down the candles and start a fire. She wouldn't be gone long, anyway.

Betsy went out into the hall and backed right into something solid, and warm. Betsy yelled out, turned and shined the flashlight right into the face of Maya Pineda. Her hair hung in wet strands and her arms were full of manila folders bursting with paper.

"Oh, so sorry, Maya," Betsy said. "You're home early."

Maya squinted and turned her face away from the light.

"Do you mind—"

THE DARK SIDE OF THE ROOM

Betsy moved the flashlight away as the woman knelt down to pick up some paper that had fallen.

"Power's out all over," Maya said, stuffing pages back into a folder.

Betsy watched Maya carefully, and counted the number of buttons done up on her blouse. When she'd left for work this morning, Maya had every button fastened except the top. Now there were two others undone, enough to see the lace of her black bra.

"So, no late work tonight?" Betsy asked, trying to sound innocent.

Maya stood and shifted the massive stack in her arms.

"I didn't bring all this home for safekeeping," she said.

Oh, she is a B-minor, Betsy thought. She hated the word, but here it fit. Maya Pineda was young, with smooth skin and raven-black hair. And she was pretty, beautiful even. A paralegal with some ambulance chaser's firm, and Betsy believed Miss Pineda probably earned most of her salary bent over a desk. As if the undone buttons and frequent late nights didn't tell the whole story.

Thunder vibrated through the walls. Maya jerked

and it gave Betsy a little jolt of satisfaction.

"Your mascara's running," Betsy said, and pointed briefly with the flashlight. Maya hissed and closed her eyes.

Betsy moved the beam to the apartment two doors down from hers.

"A new guy moved into Campbell's old place," she said. "Weird fellow, didn't speak at all. I think he's mute."

"Let's hope for his sake he's deaf too," Maya said, as she struggled to keep her grip on the folders. "I've got to get inside."

Maya walked away without saying goodnight, and Betsy thought again about what a B-minor she was. The kind of woman best kept away from other women's husbands. Pencil skirt and high heels. Who wears high heels except someone expecting men to watch her leave a room? Betsy almost spit onto the frayed and dirty carpet, but stopped herself. She didn't like thinking of other people this way, but something about Maya Pineda rubbed her the wrong way, so to speak. And that comment about the new guy being deaf, that was probably about Betsy's piano playing. She was no Phineas Priest, but she wasn't bad. And if it bothered Maya, why hadn't she said anything before?

That's what B-minors do. They don't say anything

and let the anger fester until it comes spilling out. B-minors were volcanoes in Betsy's opinion.

After Maya went inside her apartment across the hall, Betsy walked down to the apartment next to hers and knocked on the door. She heard jazz music playing on the other side. Must be a vinyl on that battery powered record player Jerry sometimes took on camping trips. Never without his music, Jerry.

It was Greg who opened the door. He held a half-full glass of red wine, and he smiled big when he saw Betsy.

"Bets," he said, "come on in. Join us."

"Oh, if it's not too much trouble," she said.

"Jer," Greg called behind him, "look what the cat dragged in."

Betsy laughed, because the joke wasn't meant to be hurtful, and it didn't hurt. They, and they alone, knew just how many cats she had. And the fact that they'd kept her secret from Al, and the rest of the residents, made her grateful. It had been a point of contention with Kristy, and that *was* something that hurt.

Jerry rose from the couch, wobbled a little, and made his way to her, bare feet slapping on the hardwood floor. Then he wrapped his arms around her in a hug and kissed her cheek. She smelled the wine on his breath, heard it in his speech.

"Kind of exciting isn't it?" he asked. "We were just talking about what we'd do if the power never came back on."

Greg came over and gently guided Jerry back to the couch. A propane lantern sat on the coffee table and gave the room some light.

"You were talking about it," he said, "I was just listening."

Yes, they were gay, but that didn't bother Betsy in the slightest. In fact, she found it sort of fascinating because they were nothing like what she imagined a gay couple would be. At least nothing like what they showed on TV. Jerry was black and Greg was white, and she knew that Greg's family had not taken either revelation very well, which somehow made her feel better about her own situation. Neither of them was particularly flamboyant, and they were both middle-aged, attractive men. Could probably have their pick of women, if they wanted. And they'd have the good sense to avoid Maya Pineda, if they were straight. She knew they would.

Greg wore an unbuttoned red flannel shirt with the

sleeves rolled up, and Betsy could just make out the shadow of his muscles on the T-shirt underneath. He waved Betsy inside and offered her a glass of wine, which she declined. Better than liquor or beer, anyway, but she still didn't agree with the consumption of alcohol. Made people stupid, in her opinion.

Betsy realized her flashlight was still on, so she turned it off to preserve battery. Greg motioned to a modern, and uncomfortable looking chair. Betsy sat without actually leaning back into it. She stayed on the edge, hands folded in her lap the way her mother had taught her, and the way she taught Kristy.

"The lobby is leaking again," Betsy said, and she noticed how differently her voice echoed in this apartment. Must be the floors. She still had mostly carpet, easier to clean with cats. On hardwood the fur just blew all over the place anytime the door opened, or someone walked through the room. Carpet, at least, could be vacuumed easily.

"I'm sure Al will get right on that," Jerry said, and laughed. A drunk laugh, Betsy noted, and although his was carefree she still didn't like the slightly unhinged quality his voice took on.

Jerry was the younger of the two, but not by much. You couldn't really tell physically, but his age was apparent in his personality, in the way he was always smiling, always looking at the world through bright eyes. Greg was the more serious of the two, and Betsy loved the way Jerry was constantly trying to make him laugh.

Greg sat down next to Jerry, put his arm around his partner's shoulders, and took a drink of wine.

"How's the crew handling the blackout?" he asked.

She liked that Greg called her cats the "crew," like together they were some kind of gang, and not something weird or disgusting.

"It bothers them some, but they'll be alright," Betsy said, feeling her hands start to sweat.

Jerry leaned his head into Greg's chest and smiled. "I keep trying to convince him to let me get a dog," he said. "But," he puffed his lips out and deepened his voice, "we're not home enough to be good pet owners. It would be unfair to the animal."

Betsy smiled in spite of herself as Greg gently slapped the side of Jerry's head. It was a good impression, and a kindhearted one. Not like the ones the kids on the third floor did of her. Thank God no children were allowed on the fourth floor. Part of the reason was the second half of this floor had been damaged in a fire and never repaired. Al put up a makeshift wall just down beyond Campbell's old place, where the new, weird resident now lived.

Betsy swallowed hard. She wasn't sure why she got nervous around other people sometimes, couples mostly, but she did and there was nothing she could to do to stop it from happening.

"I wanted to ask, did either of you meet the new tenant?" Betsy asked.

Jerry sat up a little, looked into his empty glass, and reached for the wine bottle.

"No," he said. "Al found someone already?"

"He's kind of strange," Betsy said. "I think maybe he's disabled or something."

Greg's blue eyes stared at her, and they made her feel a little funny. She had once described him to a friend she played bridge with once a week, and the word that kept coming to mind was "present." As in, Greg is present is whatever moment he's living in. He makes you think he cares, and what a gift that is.

"Disabled how?" Greg asked.

"He didn't say a word for one thing. I think he's

mute but he understood me fine. At least I think he did. And the way he walked, even the way he stood," Betsy shivered a little at the memory of the strange ripples that moved over the man's body, "it just looked painful. Like he couldn't quite stand straight."

Greg nodded and handed his glass to Jerry for a refill.

"Another thing," Betsy said, "he smelled real bad, like he hadn't bathed in a long time. And there were scratches all over his face, nasty looking ones."

Greg and Jerry exchanged a glance.

"Here we go again," Jerry said.

"I don't think he's using drugs," Betsy said, but as soon as the words left her mouth she realized she had no reason to feel that way. How would she know whether the man was an addict or not? In fact, everything about him suggested he was on something strong, something that dulled the world and made him invincible to any pain he might feel as a result of his condition.

"I was thinking," Betsy said, "we should all take him a housewarming gift or something, that way you could meet him, see what you think."

Jerry opened his mouth but Greg put a hand on

his leg, and said, "That's a great idea. It would be a good opportunity for us to meet our new neighbor, find out a little bit more about him."

Betsy smiled, and continued smiling as Jerry talked about a set he was designing for a production at Portland Center Stage, but she couldn't stop thinking about their strange new neighbor and how unsettled he had made her feel. She couldn't shake the feeling that he wasn't really there, that she had finally lost her mind (just like Kristy was always afraid she'd do) and had seen a phantom. And now, here she was telling other people what she'd seen, not even knowing she was demonstrating her own loss of reality.

Jerry laughed at something, and Betsy laughed along, but she wasn't sure who said what or why it was funny. All she could hear were her own thoughts, and they were screaming about how badly she didn't want to find out anything more about the new neighbor. In fact, she wished that he'd never moved in at all.

3

When Betsy left their apartment she felt a little better, though she couldn't say why. Maybe it was because Greg and Jerry were so kind, and kindness was a thing that seemed so rare in this world. And it shined all the brighter when you found it.

Betsy was about to go back to her place, make sure the cats hadn't lit the couch on fire, when she smelled marijuana smoke drifting down the hallway, which meant Devin was home. She turned on the flashlight and made her way to his apartment. The smell was stronger in front of his door, and Betsy imagined him sitting alone in the dark, the burning end of his joint the only light in the room.

Devin worked the night shift down at the docks,

loading and unloading shipping containers. Everything from Japanese cars to crates of canned tomatoes—if it came through Portland, Devin was probably the one who moved it from ship to shore. Because it took so long to get used to working graveyard, Devin would stay up all night even on his days off. "A nocturnal creature," he once called himself. And it was true. He slept during the day and worked in the dark. He was a Grumpy Gus if Betsy had ever met one, and she was sure it was because he lived in a backwards world.

She lifted her hand and was about to knock but something stopped her. A sound. Faint and distant. It was a fast sound, and she knew that didn't make any sense but it was the first word that came to mind. The noise of something moving quickly, and it made her think of her father doing woodwork in their garage when Betsy was just a girl. He had a long, metal tool full of ridges that always reminded her of a cheese grater, and he would use to file down the edges of splintery boards. Back and forth, dragging those ridges over the wood with a chattering sound.

This was like that, but the wood had a low sound and this was high, the click of hard things, like a woman tapping long nails on her teeth in rapid succession. And it wasn't just one thing making this sound, it was dozens, if not more.

Insects, was her next thought. Grasshoppers rubbing those serrated legs together. But that wasn't quite right either.

She put her ear to Devin's door and listened. Quiet. Not even the creak of a floor.

Betsy turned the flashlight to the hallway past Devin's room. There was another door, Campbell's old apartment, occupied now by the strange, new man with the crooked body. And not far beyond his door was the wall Al had built. Still just plywood, a few stray pieces of sheetrock. How the thing stayed up was a mystery to her. Al's laziness knew no limits, and this wall, if you could even call it that, stood as a monument to his ineptitude as a superintendent, and maybe even as a human. There were large gaps between the makeshift wall and the real walls on either side of the hallway. A musty draft blew from the gaps, tinted with the smell of burned wood. There were rooms on the other side of Al's wall. Boarded up, abandoned. Most with the charred remains of furniture and belongings still in them.

All the tenants on that end of the hall had already moved into hotels before the fire because of a bad roof leak that had caused mold to start growing in the apartments. A remediation crew was scheduled to come and clean things up just a few days after the fire started.

Betsy wasn't really distressed about the fire because she had walked down there one day not long before it had burned, and she'd seen dozens of spider webs and egg sacks in the hallway, crisscrossed over the doors.

There were three creatures Betsy despised more than any others: rats, cockroaches, and spiders. The world would be better off without them, she thought.

Al had promised everyone he was going to hire contractors to repair the fire damage, and then bring in new residents. But for whatever reason, he still hadn't done it. Greg said it probably had something to do with the insurance money, but Betsy didn't know enough about insurance to have an opinion one way or the other.

Betsy turned and started to make her way back home when she caught a fresh whiff of Devin's joint. Oh, how she hated that smell. Like a compost heap caught on fire. She breathed deep, straightened her sweatshirt with one hand, and knocked twice on Devin's door.

THE DARK SIDE OF THE ROOM

The creak of couch cushions from inside. Feet padding on the floor. The deadbolt slid back, the door opened, and the pale face that appeared hissed "shit" and held a hand up over his eyes.

Betsy said, "Oh, sorry," and quickly turned off the flashlight. "Good evening, Devin. I hope I'm not bothering you."

"Blinding me, yes. Bothering me, no." Devin said.

With no light the entire hallway was as black as covering your head with a blanket in a dark room, but as her eyes adjusted, Betsy could see the orange glow of Devin's joint on the coffee table and the slowly coiling silver strands of smoke rising from it.

Devin stood leaning in the doorway, rubbing his face and sniffing. "What do you want, Betsy?"

"Did you…" Betsy started, but stopped herself. The question she was going to ask, nothing but a few simple words, was an echo she recognized from a long time ago. Who was the first to ask it? Robert? Kristy? Her therapist? The psychologist? Maybe they'd all asked her at one time or another, and Betsy did not want to make her mouth form the words, but she could think of no other way to say it.

"Did you hear anything…strange?" she asked.

Devin laughed a little, which set off a coughing fit. Betsy felt spittle touch her cheeks, and she took a step back.

"I'm hearing the rain," Devin said. "Nothing but big fat drops of water, enough to drown the whole world." He straightened up, crossed his arms, and said, "But that's not what you meant."

"Something in the walls," Betsy whispered, and she wasn't sure why she did. She tried to replicate the sound by moving her tongue against her teeth, but her mouth was dry and it sounded nothing like what she heard.

Devin suddenly backed away into the room and hurried over to the coffee table where his joint sat in an ashtray. He picked it up, waved an arm at Betsy to come in, and took a drag. Silver smoke poured out of his mouth. Betsy put a hand over her nose and stepped inside. Moonlight streamed in through an open window and fell on the floor in a slanted rectangle, illuminating a puddle of water that sparkled.

"Cockroaches," Devin said, falling backward onto the couch. "I hear them all the time, scratching and nibbling. Since Al hasn't done shit about the other rooms, those little fuckers have probably taken over."

THE DARK SIDE OF THE ROOM

Betsy winced at his use of the "F-word" but held her tongue. Devin was a blue-collar man, and he spoke in blue-collar language. Betsy scolding him wouldn't change that, but still, the word made her skin crawl.

"I've never heard any cockroaches," Betsy said. She could see Devin more clearly in the moonlit room, his skinny, bare arms and sharp nose. When he took another drag from the joint his eyes glowed with the orange light.

Devin coughed once, and holding the joint gently between two fingers, said, "If we all dropped our nukes and vaporized civilization, those things would survive and rule the earth."

Of course, cockroaches would never dare to intrude on her space. She shared living quarters with over two dozen guardians who would protect her from the disgusting insects. Still, the thought of those creatures with their sleek, shiny armor and antennae, creeping through the walls, chewing up whatever they could find, translucent larvae bursting out of eggs, not to mention all the poo... she had to swallow hard to keep her gag reflex from getting triggered.

Devin set down the joint and went over to the open window. He stood in the center of the growing puddle in bare feet and looked outside.

"Listen," he said. He held up one hand and tilted his head.

Betsy listened, but didn't hear anything besides the rain.

"The drops," Devin said, "they hit cars and mailboxes and trashcans and puddles and leaves."

His right hand started making motions in the air, waving back and forth like a conductor.

"And they all make different sounds. It's a symphony."

The Devin she knew did not care about things such as nature and beauty, but then again, she had never had a conversation with Devin while he was getting high. Personally, she never thought of marijuana as medicine, but maybe for some people it was. Devin was not nearly as high strung or grouchy as she expected, but still, she never much cared for conversing with people she knew to be altered. It made her nervous, made her feel as though she were the only one experiencing the moment. At least, the moment that was actually happening.

She slowly backed away toward the still open door.

"We have a new neighbor," she said. "Well, he's

actually your neighbor. He's in Campbell's old place. Have you met him yet?"

Devin continued looking out the window. "I've heard movement," he said. "Someone walking. Moving things."

As Betsy walked backwards, she noticed, not for the first time, how bare Devin's apartment was. One couch, one table, one TV. No plants, no bookshelves, not even a stereo. She wondered if he saved all the money he made, or if he spent it on booze and whores as soon as he cashed the check.

Whores. That wasn't fair at all. She had never seen him bring a male friend over, let alone a woman.

Stop judging, Betsy Lupino.

"He's a strange fellow," Betsy said, near the door now.

Devin stretched his hand into the outside air, let rain fall into his palm.

"I don't give a shit as long as he's quiet."

"I think he's mute," Betsy said.

Devin pulled his hand back in and looked at the water collected there.

"Wonderful," he said.

Betsy stepped into the hall and gently closed the door behind her.

4

Betsy made it back to her apartment and stopped with her hand on the doorknob. She heard a voice, upset, talking low. She tiptoed over to Maya's door and the voice was clearer now, moving back and forth across the room. Her footsteps were quiet, which meant she'd kicked the heels off.

"You know how many times I've heard that?" Maya said. "No. No, you listen. I believed you, but all you've done is lie and string me along. I'm finished."

Betsy's eyebrows went up. Good for her, the hussy had some chutzpah after all, and Betsy didn't need to be a detective to know who Miss Pineda was talking to. Her boss, most likely. One of those bigwig lawyers in a suit that cost more than Betsy's monthly rent.

Maya went silent for a few seconds, then her voice rose again and Betsy felt a little guilty for listening, so she backed away to her door.

Thankfully, the cats hadn't burned the place down. The candles still flickered, and her animals cast giant black shadows on the walls. Topsy and Evelyn were both curled on top of the baby grand, and normally Betsy would play a few tunes before bed (lullabies she used to sing for Kristy when she was just a girl) but it was late and Betsy was tired, so she decided to wash up, brush her teeth, and get some sleep. The litter boxes could wait until morning.

She cupped her hand around one of the candles, blew gently and winced at the small burst of pain when melted wax hit her skin. She touched each cat, spoke their names and said goodnight. She came to the candle on top of the piano, blew it out, and shivered a little when that whole corner of the room fell into darkness. There was only one left now, an orange halo of light that sat on the dining room table. An old, scarred table covered in rolls of yarn and half made caps for all the preemie infants at the hospital. Betsy scolded herself for placing a candle in such a dangerous place. One brush of a cat's tail and the yarn would have sparked to flame and burned the place down.

Oh well, no sense in beating yourself up over what didn't happen.

Still, Betsy told herself she needed to be more careful. What would Kristy have said if she saw that? One more reason Betsy couldn't visit Jules. And even though Betsy knew there was no hope of seeing her granddaughter, she did hope all the same. What sense was there in living without hope?

Betsy shuffled over to the still open window and breathed in rain-scented air. Devin was right, the sound of the water really did sound like a symphony. She listened for thunder and heard nothing but rain running down the gutters, dripping from the fire escape and making noise like small bells.

A shape jumped up into the window sill and startled Betsy. She cried out, took a step backward, and bumped into the dining room table. The orange halo of candlelight wobbled along the wall and ceiling, and Betsy turned just in time to grab it, stop it from falling over. With the candle righted, Betsy looked back to the window and saw Shadow sitting there, his tail moving in slow, gentle motions. Something hung limply from his mouth. His eyes glowed in the faint light. The thing was black, folded between his jaws. She thought it was a sock at first, something Shadow picked up from one of the trashcans in the alley, but it was too thick to be a sock. And what was the long thin thing at one end?

Betsy made a soothing sound and reached out to take whatever Shadow had brought her, but his mouth opened before she could touch it and the thing fell to the floor with a thud. Betsy picked up the candlestick and knelt down to take a closer look. When the orange halo fell on the thing, Betsy took a quick, sharp breath. One hand went to her sweatshirt, where her heart would be. The fur of the thing was dark and wet, not just with rainwater, but with bright red blood that was slowly leaking from the puncture wounds in its side. That long, thin thing? That was a tail, a disgusting, hairless tail. The one eye she could see was still open but staring lifelessly. Its big yellow teeth protruded from a whisker-covered snout.

This wasn't just a rat. It was the biggest, ugliest rat Betsy Lupino had ever seen. She looked back up at the window, but Shadow was already gone. Back into the night.

She leaned down, candlestick in hand, to get a closer look at the rodent. It was nearly as big as some of her smaller cats like Shasta and Evelyn, and that wet and bloody fur made her stomach flutter like when the contestant she was rooting for on *Jeopardy* got the wrong answer.

Betsy needed it out of the house. Immediately. She couldn't stand the sight of it any longer. She loved nearly all animals, but rodents in particular made her skin crawl and her armpits sweat. Lizards she could handle. Even snakes, if they were small enough. But spiders, roaches, and rodents got under her skin in a way she couldn't explain. Things like that weren't a choice, it was something you were born with. Everyone was programmed to hate certain things, and rats were one of those for Betsy Lupino.

But this rat was dead. There was nothing to worry about. So Betsy leaned in closer, studying the way that slick fur laid on the creature's back, as if run through with a comb. The small holes in its side where blood leaked out, those made heat bloom up Betsy's neck. She could see angry flesh through the coarse black fibers.

The eyes, small, black, and round—like the heads of the pins she used to measure fabric around Kristy's tiny frame to make a Sunday dress when she was just a girl. And the claws, especially the back ones, they looked like the fingers of an arthritic old woman. Hairless and gnarled with long nails. Part of her wanted to touch one, just to see what it felt like, but her scalp itched at the thought. So she leaned in even closer, bent the candle so far that wax dripped down the side and hardened before it reached her finger. Nasty claws. Devin was wrong. This was the source of the sound she heard near Campbell's old place, no doubt about it. Dozens of those claws scratching in the walls.

Betsy's face was so close she could smell the creature. She wrinkled her nose at the strong ammonia odor that made her think of a bathroom that hadn't been cleaned in a long time. The tail, long and pinkish brown, looked like a big worm attached to the rat's body. Maybe she hated that tail most of all. A cat's tail was soft and comforting, the way it curled around her leg as Starry walked by. But this, this was a thing dragged through feces and urine and rotting garbage. Betsy's stomach did a little flip-flop and she decided to get rid of the thing.

Her eyes watered some from the odor, and the rat was blurred to a smear of black. Then the back claw closest to her face moved. It twitched and the claws scraped the floor with a small, terrible sound. Betsy yelled and scrambled backwards, knocking over the candle which

THE DARK SIDE OF THE ROOM

winked out.

"Fiddlesticks," Betsy said, out loud. "Fiddlesticks and C-minor."

When Kristy was young, Betsy had taught her to say piano chords instead of curse words when she was angry, or hurt. Kristy grew to hate the childishness of it, but Betsy had never stopped using them.

The apartment was completely dark except for the faint glow of a street lamp outside. Betsy couldn't tell where the rat was, and she hoped to God that it was only nerves that moved its claw, that it wasn't alive enough to get up and scurry through her home.

She put her free hand on one leg and groaned as she rose. Her eyes slowly adjusted and she could see the lump of fur still on the ground. Waving her hands back and forth, and shuffling her feet, Betsy walked to the kitchen where the lighter was.

"It's okay, guys," Betsy said to the cats. "I'll get us light in two shakes and then we'll dispose of that thing."

She turned and saw a shape moving out of the shadows towards the rat. She couldn't tell which cat it was, but Betsy stomped her foot and hissed.

"Leave that alone," she said.

The cat slunk back into the dark. Betsy made it to the kitchen, got the lighter, and went back to the window. The ammonia smell seemed stronger now as Betsy lit the candle. It illuminated a large misshapen hunk of wax on the floor and Betsy whispered, "G flat major."

The rat was no longer moving, but that did not make Betsy feel any better. She took the candle back into the kitchen, slipped on her dishwashing gloves, and grabbed a trash bag from under the sink.

Betsy set the candle on the table and stood over the creature, bag in one hand. Now, how to pick it up? Grab it by the middle and feel its body squish in her hand? Pinch one claw between two fingers, or…the tail? Betsy shivered once and swallowed hard. The tail would be best, but good Lord she did not want to touch it. Eyes closed, then.

Betsy bent down, her yellow-gloved fingers reaching out, and once they were close she shut her eyes. Even through the gloves she could feel the hard stubbiness of the tail and she tasted bile. She pinched hard, tried not to think of the thing suddenly springing to life and trying to squirm away, and lifted the rodent up. It was heavy, much heavier than she expected. And the smell rose with the creature as she lifted it up into the bag. She squinted her eyes open to make sure it went inside, then she twisted the top again and again, until she was certain it couldn't jump out.

Betsy went over to the window and leaned out. Gentle rain fell on her face and it felt good. Four stories below her was the narrow alley where the garbage cans were kept. If Al was any good at his job, the cans would be well-kempt and lined up. But he wasn't, so they were knocked over half the time and stray animals ripped open the bags, dug through all the old food and diapers. She hoisted the bag, gave it a couple swings, and let it sail out past the fire escape railing. It disappeared as it fell, and Betsy listened until she heard a faint thump from below.

She nodded once, pulled herself back inside, and took the gloves off inside-out. Into the trash with those. She'd have to remember to buy a new pair next time she was at the grocery store. When she turned around, ten glowing eyes were watching her from various points in the room.

"All clear, folks," she said, and her voice had a shake in it. A shake she didn't like one bit. "Listen, you keep the rats away, alright? You don't bring them in here. Shadow didn't know better, but I'll have a talk with him."

Some of the eyes blinked.

TYLER JONES

A sudden wave of fatigue fell over Betsy and she wanted nothing more than to get in bed and fall asleep. She grabbed the candle and started toward her bedroom, but she stopped briefly, as she always did, at the picture of her and Kristy. She smiled to herself, remembering what it felt like to love and be loved. She was about to keep moving when she noticed that the dark corner of the room near the piano seemed to be moving. She held the candle up above her head and walked toward the piano. Light fell on the corner and nothing was there, but that didn't stop Betsy from lying awake in bed most of the night.

5

In the morning the rain stopped. The sky was still gray and full of dark clouds, but Portland was mostly like that in the fall whether it rained or not. After a hot shower, Betsy filled the five large bowls on the floor with cat food, made herself a breakfast of eggs, toast, and tea, then sat at the piano. She lifted the fallboard and placed her fingers on the keys. Was it just her imagination, or did her hands look older every time she sat down to play? Veins bulged like blue worms under her skin, and her knuckles seemed swollen.

Old lady hands, she thought.

Betsy Lupino closed her eyes and began to play a Phineas Priest song she had memorized. She played softly to be courteous to her neighbors, even though no one had ever complained. Priest was her favorite jazz musician, a notoriously reclusive pianist who, in his later years, would speak to no one but his wife. He even conducted entire studio sessions through Patrice. She would tilt her head close to her husband's mouth, listen, then communicate his instructions to the rest of the band. What a brilliant, troubled mind.

Dementia, probably. Maybe even Alzheimers, or a brain tumor. Something that twisted his thoughts into incredible sounds, but rendered him unable to perform even simple tasks without getting stressed and anxious.

The song came flowing out of the piano, a haunting, melancholy melody that comforted Betsy because it seemed to say something about being alive that she didn't have words for.

Minor keys were what made a sad song, sad. Those dark chords gave pain and heartache a sound. The notes floated and dove, hovered and fell, and one by one the cats emerged from their hiding places. They slinked from the couch, the bedroom and bathroom, from under the armchair and off the dresser. Topsy and Turvy (brother and sister) liked to sleep in the closet, and they came out through the cracked open door.

When Betsy felt several rub against her legs, she opened her eyes and began to count. As usual Shadow was the only one missing. But she didn't expect him. He came and went as he pleased.

Betsy did this every morning. It was her way of taking stock of what she had. She loved each and every one of those cats, and counting them reminded her of what the world had not yet taken away.

When the song finished, Betsy covered the keys and picked up Shasta, the fat orange tom with white spots. He purred into her neck as she stroked his back. She knew what he was saying, just as Patrice knew what Phineas Priest said.

Shasta said to her, *this is all I need.*

6

The power was back on, so at 10 A.M. Betsy turned the TV on and let it drone in the background while she knitted a pink infant cap for the hospital. The cats lazed, used the litter box, and played with each other on one of the four cat towers positioned throughout the apartment.

The morning news showed a reporter in a blue rain jacket standing in the middle of a residential street. Behind him were several cop cars parked to block off traffic. The reporter pointed to a black circle of melted asphalt and talked about a man who had been lit on fire during the night. The victim was taken to Emmanuel hospital where he died a few hours later.

Betsy shook her head as the reporter interviewed

some of the people who lived on Archer Way. This victim was just the latest in series of arson attacks.

She couldn't understand the world anymore, not that she could before the dark took up residence in her head, but it just all seemed so awful these days. Worse than it ever was.

The news faded into a talk show, which faded into a soap opera, and then reruns of an old sitcom. Betsy hardly paid attention. She kept thinking about Kristy, about how her head had once been small enough to fit inside this tiny cap. And now…now she was grown and her head was big and she had a daughter of her own Betsy was not allowed to see. How unfair the world was. She sometimes wondered if it turned backward instead of forward. Took everything good and spun it back into ruin.

By late afternoon the rain had started again and Betsy had to refill the food bowls. She shuffled through the kitchen in her slippers with the rubber soles. No way was she going to slip and fall like Nadine Dempsey from the second floor. A broken hip and a ticket to a memory care facility is where that got her.

Betsy opened the cupboards and was struck by the fact that she had more cat food than human food.

THE DARK SIDE OF THE ROOM

She opened the refrigerator and was surprised she hadn't noticed earlier how empty it was. A trip to the store, then. Was that becoming a daily occurrence? She thought it was. As soon as she stepped foot inside the grocery store just a few blocks from her apartment, Betsy's head went completely blank in the all the fluorescent lights and brightly colored packaging—and she forgot what she went there for in the first place. Half the time she came back home with bags full of items she didn't need, or even want, but none of the things she actually needed.

She told herself it was just part of getting older and living alone, but a deeper part told her something inside was slowly slipping away.

Betsy shook her head, saw the food bowls again and remembered what she was doing, where she was going. She slipped on a sweater, wrapped her mostly white hair into a bun, and laced up a pair of waterproof boots that were not only warm, but gripped the slick sidewalks and tiled floors of the grocery store. By the time she put on her jacket, Betsy could already feel a thin trickle of sweat sliding down her back.

"I'll be back soon," she said to the cats.

She looked over to open window, which she kept

that way for Shadow, and hoped he wouldn't bring home another surprise. She left the apartment and went down the stairwell, feeling a grind in her hip with each step, but it wasn't too painful and she kept one hand on the railing. When she reached the lobby, that trickle of sweat was now a creek that made her feel like she needed another shower.

Maya Pineda was in the lobby checking her mailbox, and Betsy was surprised to find she no longer thought of the woman as a B-minor.

"Good morning," Betsy said.

Maya spun around. Her eyes narrowed and her lips tightened when she saw Betsy.

"Morning."

Betsy walked past, through an invisible cloud of her neighbor's perfume, and found it oddly pleasant. She hated most scents, but this one was sweet and tropical and it mixed well with Maya's skin.

Betsy's hand was on the front door and she started to push it open, then stopped and turned around.

"Does my piano playing bother you?" Betsy asked.

Maya's mouth fell open a little. Her eyes widened.

She started to shake her head, "No, why would you—" She stopped, nodded. "Oh, what I said last night?"

Betsy lifted her eyebrows.

Maya sighed, closed the metal door of her mailbox with a clang.

"I'm sorry," she said. "I was in a bad mood. Things haven't been easy at the office. So bad, in fact, I quit my job last night."

She lifted a handful of envelopes.

"But these will keep on coming. Lawyers talk, you know? Word gets around and I may not be able to find another job."

There was a cold pocket of air in Betsy's chest, and it burned as it moved up into her throat. She hated that she had judged Maya so harshly, knowing next to nothing about her. They'd been neighbors for what, two, three years? And Betsy had never so much has had an actual conversation with the woman.

"It's sad, isn't it?" Betsy said. "How the word that gets around is usually a lie? And the truth can't run fast enough to catch up."

Maya laughed, and it was a beautiful, musical sound. Not a minor note at all, but a major one. *E probably*, Betsy thought.

It struck Betsy that Maya was probably as old as

Kristy, and that made the cold pocket of air vanish.

Think of her as your own. As someone you love.

Betsy smiled her best motherly smile, which was out of practice, but Maya smiled back.

"I'm sure you'll find something in no time," Betsy said. "You're hardworking and dedicated. That's rare these days. Any firm would be lucky to have you."

Was it Betsy's imagination or were Maya's eyes filling with tears?

"Thank you," Maya said.

Betsy turned to leave and stopped again.

"Have you had any issues with rats lately?" she asked.

Maya tilted her head. "Do you mean men, or actual rats?"

Betsy said, "Shadow came home with one last night, and earlier I thought I heard something in the walls down near Campbell's old place."

"Shadow?"

"He mostly lives outdoors, but he comes home for food and love when he get hungry or lonely."

Maya laughed again. "Oh, he's a cat!"

Betsy's felt her cheeks go hot with blood rush. She

nodded. "Big gray one. You've probably seen him sneaking around on the fire escapes. He'll scratch at your window, but don't let him in. He's a beggar, that one."

Maya made her beautiful face look mock serious. "Duly noted. No food for Shadow."

"He's picky," Betsy added. "You'll go through the trouble of getting him something and he won't eat it. Every cat likes tuna except Shadow. Too many years eating out of trash cans, I guess."

Maya's phone buzzed, but she ignored it. "How many cats do you have?"

The heat moved up Betsy's cheeks and into her scalp, which now itched.

"Four," she said, without thinking, and sweat immediately ran down her neck.

"Wow," Maya said. "That's a lot."

"Oh, they're easy," Betsy said. "They mostly just lie around and—"

Maya's phone buzzed again, and Betsy suddenly felt self-conscious. Something she had not felt in a long time. Here she was, having a conversation with a beautiful, intelligent woman and all she could talk about her were cats. But she couldn't even do that honestly. Why? Shame, probably. That's what Kristy would say. Shame that the cats were all she had in the world. Shame that she had so many of them, and so few people would understand why. It was no problem for a woman to have six pairs of shoes, but six pets and you were loony tunes.

Betsy waved a hand. "I should let you go."

The phone buzzed again and Maya shrugged. "Probably the old boss wanting me back."

"Only if it comes with a huge raise," Betsy said, and laughed a little too loudly at her own joke. Thankfully, Maya laughed too and the women said goodbye and went their separate ways.

Outside, the cool fall and rain-scented streets reminded Betsy why she loved this city, especially this time of year. Halloween decorations hung in the windows of shops she passed. Grinning jack 'o' lanterns and dancing skeletons. Cardboard cutouts of vampires with sharp fangs dripping bright red blood. A werewolf, a masked killer with a machete. The holiday was only a few days away. She'd have to remember to buy some bags of candy to give out to the kids in the apartment. She loved seeing their costumes and painted faces. Their sweet, high-pitched voices as they sang out "Trick or treat!"

THE DARK SIDE OF THE ROOM

Kristy had been a mermaid one year, that much Betsy could remember. But it saddened her that she couldn't find any memories of other characters or mythical creatures her daughter had dressed up as.

Must be on the dark side of the room, Betsy thought. *Hidden where I can't find it.*

Betsy stopped walking and put a hand against the cool brick of the building next to her. She closed her eyes and went into the Memory Room. It wasn't a real place, a location she'd ever been to. Instead, it was the kind of room she'd always wanted, in a house she'd never build. It was bright, for one thing. Massive windows filled two of the four walls and let in the light. Betsy was younger in this room. Thinner, with auburn hair and smooth skin. She wore the yellow dress and white shoes she'd been wearing when Robert had proposed.

There was a fireplace, along with a couch and a couple of chairs facing it. This was where she sat and went through old photographs. Only they weren't photographs at all. They were snapshots from her memory. Moments that her eyes shutter-closed on and captured. They appeared in this room as objects she could touch, caress. But that was before the dark came in.

How long had it been? Eight years, maybe longer?

Just a shadow at first, small and insignificant, that crept in on the far side of the room where Betsy kept her chests full of treasured items from her marriage, from being a mother. She didn't think anything of the shadow when it first arrived. It only covered a small patch of floor. But over time it had grown taller, longer, and soon it had risen up to the ceiling. A dark wall that moved forward by centimeters every couple of months. Before Betsy realized it, the shadow touched the wooden chest that contained her wedding dress and the shape and feel of her husband's hands vanished from her memory. At least there was still one photograph of her and Robert hanging near the fireplace. They stood on a beach, smiling. He had one arm around her shoulder, and her arms were wrapped around his waist. An anniversary, maybe.

Other things had gone missing since then. Important things. And now Betsy could not remember any Halloween with her daughter except the one where she dressed as a mermaid. Where had the other years gone?

In her mind, Betsy walked from the fireplace over to the wall of darkness. The whole room was less bright than it had been last year, that much was certain. A quarter of the room was in the dark now, and Betsy knew it wouldn't be long before there was no light at all. She knew this because she'd tried to get rid of the dark. She tore down the curtains, plugged in lamps (lamps from various places she'd lived over the years), even added more wood to the fire, but nothing worked. The light hit the wall of darkness and stopped. It couldn't penetrate or scatter it.

Betsy now stood in front of that wall, determined to go into it and find her memories of Kristy on Halloweens past. This was something she had not yet tried. She reached out a hand and touched the dark, gently. Her hand slipped into the dark and her skin began to tingle with a cold burn, like touching ice. She gritted her teeth and put her whole arm in. The burning got worse, so much worse she couldn't stop herself from crying out. She held it there until she couldn't take the pain anymore, then she yanked her arm back, afraid it would be nothing but bone as white and bare as the plastic skeletons in the store windows. Her arm was whole, but the dark still clung to her. Pieces of it fell off her skin in thick droplets, like black oil.

She couldn't hold it back any longer. Betsy put one hand to her mouth and began crying. The room slowly dissolved until Betsy was back on a Portland street littered with yellow and orange leaves. She was older again, standing in the cold, one hand still on the brick building, the other held to her mouth as tears ran down through her fingers.

She sensed someone near her, a man, approaching cautiously with his hand held out.

"Is everything okay?" he asked.

Betsy gave a weak smile and nodded.

"I'm fine," she said.

She wiped her cheeks and started walking away. She said, "Thank you," as she went.

When Betsy arrived at the grocery store she saw more ghoulish decorations, far bloodier and scarier than she remembered from when Kristy was little. She grabbed a basket and started walking the aisles, and when a voice came over the intercom to announce a sale on soda, Betsy had completed forgotten why she'd come to the store in the first place.

7

***Cats,* Betsy thought. Why else** did she ever come to the store except to get food for her cats? She had bags of the dry stuff, but she liked to buy cans of tuna and the fancy cat food, and mix it in with the hard bits of kibble she fed them every day. A treat.

She loaded up her basket with as much as she thought she could carry back to the apartment, and got in line. The checker eyed her purchases, then her, with eyes red and half-closed.

Pot smoker, Betsy thought.

Everyone seemed high these days. Inebriated. Numb. She hated it. She was never sure whether she was interacting with a person or just playing a role in some drug induced projection.

She paid for the tuna and cat food, grabbed the bags without so much as a "thank you" and went back outside. Light raindrops fell gently on her head and it felt good. Betsy walked by homeless men and women camped out in tattered tents, shopping baskets full to overflowing and covered in tarps strapped in place with bungee cords. She had to walk into the street just to get by one man whose camp took up the entire sidewalk. He sat on the ground picking through a pile of cigarette butts, carefully pulling them apart and collecting the unburned tobacco.

The rain started falling heavier, so Betsy stopped, set down one bag, and pulled up her hood. She smiled at the sound the water made, light little pops that made her think of what Devin said about the symphony. She paused at an intersection and waited for the light to turn. Across the street she saw someone dressed all in black walking with an unusual stride. Limping, tilting, righting himself, moving from side to side. His hood was up as well, and Betsy searched through her Memory Room for why this man's walk was so familiar.

She found it on a shelf near the fireplace. The scratched-up face, the silence, the smell.

THE DARK SIDE OF THE ROOM

The new resident.

Betsy slammed her knuckles into the button on the pole to make the walk-sign come on faster, and when it did she jogged across the intersection, metal cans banging into her knees. The sidewalk was mostly empty except for a few homeless holding signs and asking for change. Betsy ignored them and kept jogging, keeping her eyes on the swaying black figure one block ahead.

The handles of one plastic bag stretched as she struggled to keep up. She tightened her grip but the cans were heavy and the bag wouldn't hold for much longer. The resident made a clumsy left turn out of sight just as a man emerged from a stone doorway and stood right in front of Betsy, blocking her view. He held out one dirt covered hand, long fingernails (some of which were chipped) and said, "Got a dollar?"

Betsy tried looking past him, but the man moved from one foot to the other, a kind of dance, as he held out his hand.

"Just one dollar to help someone in need," he said.

His face was mostly hidden by a scraggly brown beard, and his skin was tanned a deep brown. He smiled and dozens of deep lines creased the corners of his eyes.

His teeth were stained and rotted.

"I don't carry cash," Betsy said. "I'm sorry." And she moved to go past him, but the man's open hand shot out and grabbed Betsy's arm. Not hard, but enough to startle her. Instinct told her she was being attacked, that this man meant to beat to her to death and steal her purse, her groceries, so she swung the bag of cans but the plastic split and spilled the cans onto the sidewalk before it had a chance to hit him.

Betsy jerked her arm from the man's grip and knelt down, started collecting her things. She put everything into the other bag, then handed the man one can of tuna.

"Here," she said. "I really have to go."

She clutched the now full bag to her chest and walked away as quickly as she could. Not fast enough to be out of earshot when the man held up the can and yelled, "What am I supposed to do with this?"

Betsy made the left onto a new street, but the resident was gone and the street was empty. Not a single person was on the sidewalk. No tents set up. No beggars. The rain pattered down through what leaves were still on the trees. The rest of the leaves were raked into beautifully colored piles on the curb. Betsy had once read a story in the news about a little boy who was hiding in one of those piles when someone drove through it, killing the boy. She couldn't see a pile of leaves without thinking about him.

She walked slower now and shifted the bag in her arms. She'd have to remember to bring her own reusable shopping bags next time. She decided to walk the rest of the block, then hang a right and come to the Parkrose from the backside. A little detour in the rain never hurt anybody. Besides, the cats weren't starving and there were no lit candles to worry about.

The buildings on her left rose up into the gray sky. Old stone, at least from the 1800s, with ornate carvings that made her imagine the city when it was new and pristine. She passed an alleyway between the stone building and the brick one next to it. She normally didn't look down alleys, they made her nervous, but she heard a sound not unlike the chittering she'd heard in the walls near Campbell's old place. What Devin had said were cockroaches.

Betsy stopped, squinted into the darkness of the alley. It was just like any other space between buildings— dark, wet, full of dumpsters and trash bags that hadn't quite made it in—but there was something else down there as well. Something moving along the ground just beyond where the light reached. A black shape about the size of a human body, lying face down and jerking like it was having a seizure. Betsy had seen her fair share of seizures at the children's hospital, and that's exactly what it looked like. Spasms, arms failing, legs kicking, then curling up and locking into place.

Betsy called out, "Hello?"

The movement stopped. So did that ratcheting sound.

Betsy took one step forward, stopped.

"Are you alright?"

The black shape began to rise, slowly, and Betsy thought at first that it was a costume of some kind being inflated. Two legs appeared, wearing pants, and grew until they hit a waist. Then the folded-over torso rose up and straightened, draped in a long black coat.

Betsy's mouth went dry, and her heartbeat felt bigger, like it had grown in size and was pushing against her ribs. The back of her legs went weak. She wanted to move, to run, but she couldn't.

The arms of the coat hung limply, but they too filled up with something, from the inside, and became solid. Soon, the shape stood upright and a head materialized, as though it was pushed up from inside the clothing, and the hood moved on its own, covered the head. It made no sense, but to Betsy it looked like a human shape had been poured into a pile of clothing on the ground.

When the transformation was complete a man stood in the alley, his back to Betsy, but she recognized the figure, the dirty clothes and black coat. She slowly backed away, the bag of cans clutched to her chest so tightly it hurt. She stepped out of the alleyway to the sidewalk and immediately put her back to the cold brick of the building, hoping he hadn't turned around and seen her.

She stayed as still as she could, listening. The chittering sound came back, quieter this time, and it had a slightly different tone. It started at a higher pitch, died down, then came back again with a lower pitch. Betsy closed her eyes for a second and could almost hear the noises as though they were in conversation with each other. Two separate groups of sounds communicating, arguing, maybe.

Betsy tried to hold the bag still but the cans shifted with a sound of clanking metal. The chittering noise stopped and Betsy held her breath. She heard footsteps shuffling in her direction, crunching through garbage and dead leaves, sloshing through the liquid runoff of rotting food.

She took shallows gasps as the footsteps drew closer, made her body as still as the statue in Pioneer Square, but her arms, tired from holding the heavy bag, started to quiver. Tremors ran up and down her muscles and all those metal cans rattled together. The plastic bag crinkled and it sounded so loud to her.

One heavy foot stepped into a puddle, and the other dragged behind it, scraping the ground. The sound was so close now that she feared the resident's head would appear around the corner any second. Betsy breathed deep and took off running down the street, both arms clamped so tightly around the bag that they started to cramp. Her run was more of a jog, and heat bloomed in her bad knee, but she did not stop to look behind her until she had turned the corner at the next block. Even then, it was only a quick glance as she caught her breath and tightened her grip on the bag. Then she was off again and she didn't stop until she reached the Parkrose Apartments. It was dark by the time she made it, and the sky ripped open and rain fell heavy now.

As she climbed the stairs, sweat running into all the

THE DARK SIDE OF THE ROOM

folds and crevices of her body, soaking her undergarments and shirt, it occurred to Betsy that she had run from the new resident, but the only place she could go was the same place that resident would also eventually return to.

8

She made it to the fourth floor, a wicked rasp in her breathing that she hadn't heard in months. Maybe because it had been that long since she'd exerted herself, but it concerned her all the same. The air wouldn't go as deep as she wanted it to, and she told herself she'd have to check the medicine cabinet to see if she still had her inhaler.

The whole way up the stairs she had tried to explain to herself what she'd seen. A rehearsal, she supposed, before she told the others on the floor. The resident had been lying face down in an alleyway. That was drug behavior if she'd ever seen it. No doubt about it. But the way he had stood up. She had no explanation for that. The best way she could describe it was as though an invisible puppeteer had suddenly pulled up on all the strings and raised him from the ground. The way it happened seemed to defy the laws of physics. He stood up without any of the normal movements she would expect from a man going from lying flat to standing.

Just thinking about made it her shiver.

She limped to the door of her apartment. She hadn't run in she couldn't remember how long, and the old knee injury had flared back up. She was sure it was swollen, and she'd have to remember to ice it once she got inside.

She paused in front of Maya's door, thought about knocking and asking to talk, but Betsy wasn't sure she had words for everything yet. She couldn't quite articulate the uneasiness she felt at the alley. Still felt, if she was honest with herself.

As she neared her apartment, Betsy heard a sound coming from inside. She put her ear to the door. Piano notes, random, discordant. She must have forgotten to turn the TV off. She listened for voices, for any other noises from a TV show. There was nothing but the piano.

She slipped her key into the deadbolt, turned it, and opened the door. The piano was louder now, and the song it played was truly awful. There was no sense of melody or timing at all. Just off-key notes being hit at odd intervals.

She pushed the door open farther, said, "Hello everyone. I'm home."

Her heart filled with air and floated up her chest, settled in her throat. When Betsy came home she was always greeted by the same scene: multiple cats sprawled out on the furniture, some licking up water from a bowl or eating, and usually one or two would make their way over to rub against her legs and inspect whatever she'd brought home.

The living room was empty. She didn't see a single cat. She stepped inside and closed the door behind her, started calling out the names of her cats, one by one. Then she saw the dark TV screen, and the piano notes kept playing. She set the bag on the floor, gently removed one can and made a fist around it, then tiptoed toward her baby grand. The sound was so much louder now, present in the room, and she mentally kicked herself for ever thinking it was the TV. Of course it wasn't. The sound was too rich and full to be coming from television speakers. Someone was here, playing her instrument.

With the curtains closed, the room was dark and

she couldn't see to the far side of the room where the piano sat. She crept forward, slowly. The black piano sat in a pocket of darkness, away from any light. The dark around it, underneath it, seemed to be moving, breathing. Betsy heard scratching noises coming between each staggered note. Oh, how she hated the wrongness of the playing. It made her teeth grind together. Each note was the exact wrong note to follow the one before it. It was like a child banging away with no idea of how its song should sound.

The dark hung like a heavy blanket, moved by the breathing of something behind it. Expanding and contracting. And for one brief moment Betsy was no longer in her apartment, but in her Memory Room, watching as the dark shuddered closer, enveloping more pieces of herself than she had to spare. There were tiny little pops in her head, the sound, she knew, of things disappearing. She couldn't identify which memories went missing, or how vital they may be, only that her head was getting lighter in ways that absolutely terrified her. She shook her head, faster and faster.

Back in the apartment, she thought, however irrationally, that the dark from the Memory Room was now here in her home. It had somehow traveled through the ether, slithered through a tear in the fabric between mind and matter, and was now crawling up the walls of the only place she felt safe. The can of tuna in her hand grew slick with sweat, and as those clashing notes continued to play, Betsy knew she had it in her to bash the intruder in the head with the can. She wouldn't hesitate, not even for a second, to put the metal edge right into the skull of this awful musician.

She inched past a framed picture hanging on the wall, a picture of her and someone else. A child. And for one brief moment, the part of Betsy's Memory Room that was not covered in darkness was all lit up, like lightning had struck just outside, and the flash washed everything of color—turned it all white, and she could not think of the little girl's name, or even who she was. Betsy knew the picture and the person in it were important, and she choked, put a hand to her mouth to stifle the sound.

Come on, come on, come on you old G-flat. Think.

The piano kept playing, and to Betsy the sound was as bad as the claws in the walls near Campbell's old place.

Think!

The flash of light faded and objects in her Room gained color and definition once more.

"Kristy," she whispered to herself. "My daughter, Kristy."

All those wrong notes banged away, and Betsy gripped the metal can tighter as she hunched over and crept silently toward the piano. Her reflection glided over the polished surface of the instrument, distorted like a fun house mirror. When she neared the bench, Betsy rose to her full height and yelled out, trying to make herself sound like a warrior with a weapon. Her arm was cocked back, ready to bash the can into the phantom pianist, but no one was there.

The piano stopped playing, and even in the darkness Betsy could see enough to tell there was no one on the bench. She turned around and twisted the knob on the lamp. A dull, warm light hit her eyes and she blinked away spots, turned back around to look at the piano and screamed in horror.

Three black shapes scurried over the piano keys, pressing them with their disgusting claws. The wet-looking fur, long tails, and round black eyes that stared at her without any emotion. Those awful, wrong notes rang out as the rodents ran across the keys, jumped down onto the bench, then onto the floor. Betsy screamed again, threw the can of tuna at one of the rats as it ran between her feet. The can smacked the floor and rolled away. Betsy backed up against the wall, arms flailing. Her feet danced as the other two rats followed the first under the couch. They emerged on the other side and climbed up the radiator to the open window sill.

Once they were outside, Betsy heard the snarl of a cat and saw Shadow tear past. The rats' squeaks turned to high pitched squeals. Betsy bent down and picked up the dented can from off the floor, then carefully went to the window, half expecting another rat, or three, to come out of the shadows and attack her.

Cool air blew in, rustled the curtains. She could still hear the rats squealing, but was it her bad ears or were they getting louder? Not just louder, but more of them? She stuck her head out the window and looked to the right. The alley was so dark she could hardly see anything but the outline of the fire escapes, and shapes, darker than dark, moving erratically over them.

No question now, there were other sounds out there. Not quite a squeak, but not a squeal either. It made her think of what a rat might sound like if it could bark. Short, raspy noises. Aggressive.

Shadow was somewhere down there, at the fire escape outside Devin's apartment, hissing and spitting. The squealing stopped and all Betsy could hear were those barking noises.

She called out, "Shadow! Come back here, right now. Shadow!"

Betsy squinted into the night, thought she could see her cat briefly, one paw swiping at something below him. Then a black cloud came rolling out of Devin's open window. It spilled onto the fire escape and broke apart into a dozen separate pieces, and the pieces made a circle around Shadow. Betsy heard his low growl, and all of those dark pieces lunged at the cat, covered his body. Shadow yelped, then let out a long, mournful howl. The sound cut through Betsy's heart.

"Shadow!" she screamed. She climbed out on to the fire escape and threw the tuna can at the dark mass that swarmed around the cat. The can clinked uselessly over the metal railing and fell into the alley.

There was so much pain in Shadow's voice now, alternating between hissing and howling.

"Leave him alone," Betsy screamed. "Get off him!"

Shadow's howl cut off quickly with a sickening

THE DARK SIDE OF THE ROOM

sound like a wet cough. The attack couldn't have lasted more than a minute, but to Betsy it felt like she stood in the cold for hours, watching as the dark overtook her cat. Her special boy. The one who preferred dangerous freedom to safe imprisonment. The one who first brought her the gift of a dead rat, as if to say, *I'll protect you.*

The dark mass spread out again and formed a line on one side of the lifeless lump. Then they moved in unison and pushed Shadow's body over the edge of the fire escape. Betsy heard the clang of a trash can, then, stillness.

Tears dripped off her chin. "Oh, Shadow. Oh, I'm so sorry."

Betsy buried her face in her hands and sobbed. When she finally looked up, the dark shapes were in a line, facing her. Watching.

The ache that burned in Betsy's chest didn't have words, but it needed to come out, somehow. She curled her fingers into fists, straightened her arms, and screamed into the night. It was just a sound at first, a guttural cry of anguish, but the longer she let it out, the more it became a war cry. Until words came.

"You are all going to hell!" she screamed. "All of you!" She took a deep breath and shouted again. "You'll burn and burn and nothing will ever stop the pain!"

9

Betsy stood in her apartment and she felt as if every muscle in her body was tense, trembling, to hold in the grief. Her still clenched hands shook. Her teeth ground together as she tried to control the emotions that washed over her. Wave after wave.

With her eyes closed, Betsy heard the *click click* of claws coming down the hall from the bedroom. Not nasty rat claws, but the soft, padded paws of her cats. Through tears, she watched as they came to her, circled around and rubbed her legs, purring. Five in all, and that odd number stabbed her heart. There had been six, and Shadow's death meant the number changed. It was no longer whole.

Finally, Betsy left her hands fall open, and as they

did the muscles in her legs went weak and she collapsed to the floor in a painful kneel. The cats gathered closer, swarming her body, crawling all over her, mewling in her ears, licking her chin and neck. She howled, not unlike Shadow had, and wailed so hard her pulse pounded in her forehead. The cats cried with her, raising their voices in unison, matching their pitch with hers. Rising and falling.

She didn't know how long she cried, but after a while she felt worn out, exhausted. She gathered Topsy, Evelyn, and Starry and held them close.

"Where were you guys?" she whispered. "Your brother needed you."

Betsy could have stayed there, surrounded by her cats, her family, until morning came, but there was a knock at the door and the sound made her body jerk. It came again, a little harder, then a voice, "Betsy? Is everything alright?"

Maya Pineda's voice.

Betsy got up off the floor, and walked over the to the door. She put her hand on the knob, pulled away, smoothed hair from her eyes and mouth, and then opened it.

Maya stood there, and her eyes grew wide and sympathetic when she saw Betsy's face. She glanced past

Betsy into the apartment, looking left and right for any sign of a threat.

"Oh, sweetie," Maya said, "are you okay?"

Looking into Maya's kind face—hard to believe Betsy ever thought of her as a B-minor—Betsy's shoulders began to shake again. Standing in front of this young, beautiful, capable woman, Betsy was suddenly very aware of her age and frailty and failing mind.

"I've lost so much," Betsy said. "It really hits me sometimes." She tapped the side of her head with a finger. "It just takes the all the good things, the beautiful thoughts. The things I want to remember. It doesn't touch the bad. That stays where it is."

Maya put a hand on Betsy's shoulder. She said, "I'm not sure I understand."

Betsy sniffed and shook her head. "It doesn't matter. We've got a big problem here, Maya."

"What?"

"Rats. Big F-sharp rats."

PART II

NOBODY HERE BUT ME, MY RISING FEARS, AND GRINDING GEARS

10

The cats had scattered just before Betsy let Maya into the apartment. Most went to the bedroom, but Starry hid in the carpeted cat tower and Turvy went under the couch. Betsy could see their eyes glowing.

Betsy made a pot of tea and told Maya the whole story, starting with seeing the resident in the alley, and ending with Shadow's death—which Betsy couldn't make it through without crying.

Maya listened, fingers laced together around a mug of steaming tea.

"Listen, hon," Maya said. "I believe you, but I just want to know that you're absolutely certain about what you saw?"

Betsy wiped her eyes on the sleeve of her sweater and nodded. Thank God she didn't wear makeup, or it would be smeared all over her face and clothes.

"Three rats," Betsy said, holding up the same number of fingers. "The size of small cats."

"We should tell Al," Maya said.

Betsy hissed through her teeth. "That worthless D-flat? He won't do anything."

Maya's perfect nails tapped the porcelain mug. "I've been hearing scratching in the walls for the last couple days. Makes sense that there are rats. Probably living in the burned section, you think?"

Betsy looked over at the photo of her daughter on the wall. How many years had she looked at that one picture? How much had her daughter changed since then? But Betsy didn't have any memories to age her own flesh and blood, no mental images to conjure up and see her as she was now, only as she had been.

"I hate rats so much," Betsy said. "God never should have made them."

Maya squinted up at the ceiling, turned her mug in a slow circle. Cat eyes glowed and blinked from various points in the room.

THE DARK SIDE OF THE ROOM

"They must be getting hungry," Maya said, "to start coming into apartments. Especially one with cats."

Betsy shook her head. "I think I know—"

Heavy footsteps came pounding up the stairwell. Staggered steps. A creak, more pounding. Betsy held a finger to her lips and tiptoed over to the door. She opened it just a crack as the footsteps reached the fourth floor and started coming down the hall.

The new resident, dressed in the same black clothes he'd been wearing when Betsy first met him, came lumbering down the hall with his strange walk. Arms and legs flailing, upper body moving side to side. He looked as though he was going to fall over with each step, but every time his head and chest pitched forward, he'd right himself.

He came closer, and his odor came with him. Rotten, sickly sweet. Betsy swallowed back the taste of tea and bile. A sound came from the man, like leather creaking but higher pitched, and she didn't see any leather clothing anywhere on him. And something was different about his face. Betsy knew her memory wasn't much these days, but she remembered faces. And this face looked nothing like what she saw in the lobby the evening she first met him.

The mouth hung open, chin almost touching

his chest, and as the resident took a step his torso flung backward, shaking the hood that covered his head and causing it slide up. Foggy, open eyes stared straight ahead.

Betsy stifled her inhale with a hand. The resident pitched forward, caught himself just before falling over, and continued lurching down the hall. Betsy had seen the face, just briefly, but enough for her to recognize the sharp nose.

Maya had gotten up and come to the door, stood just behind Betsy and looked out through the crack.

"It's him," Maya whispered.

Betsy, with one hand still covering her mouth, shook her head and whispered back, "No."

"What?" Maya said, a little too loud.

It looked like the new resident, and moved like him too. But that face was not the face Betsy remembered.

Betsy opened the door a little farther and poked her head out into the hall. Maya put a warm hand on her back, grabbed a fistful of sweater. The staggering figure in black clothes made its way to the door of Devin's apartment and lifted an arm. It stayed extended like that for a few seconds, then Betsy saw the glint of metal as a key came out of the coat sleeve. The arm swayed, stabbed forward, aiming for the lock but missing, scratching lines in the door.

Maya, taller than Betsy, leaned over her shoulder and peered down the hall as well.

"He's so drunk," she said, her breath hot against Betsy's cheek.

It seemed like it, but that answer didn't feel right to Betsy. This was more than drunk, more than being high. No, this was something worse, much worse.

She heard Maya swallow, felt the woman's eyelashes tickle her ears as she blinked.

"Oh my god."

The key finally scraped its way into the lock and turned. Then the resident went inside and closed the door behind him. Betsy closed her own door, locked it, and let out the breath she hadn't realized she'd been holding. Her chest started heaving as thoughts filled her head, crowded in there along with all the other things she didn't want to know or remember.

Maya took a few steps back, tried to laugh but coughed instead.

"You don't have any booze, do you?" she asked. "I could use a drink."

"Why does he have a key to Devin's place?" Betsy

said. She closed her eyes tight and tried to think of an explanation, but all she saw was the looming dark in her Memory Room. Growing, expanding, coming closer. The other side of that room is where answers used to be found. Dates, names, places, phone numbers, addresses, details that mattered, all lost in there, and with them, her ability to think complex thoughts, to piece things together in any meaningful way. She didn't even realize she had started crying until Maya wrapped both arms around her shoulders and pulled her into an embrace.

"It's okay," Maya said.

"Nothing makes sense," Betsy said, her voice thick with tears.

She sniffed hard and pulled away, looked into Maya's eyes.

"Please, tell me you saw him."

Maya took Betsy's hand, looked right back at her.

"I saw him," she said. "I didn't see his face, but I saw him go into Devin's apartment."

"You saw how he was walking?"

Maya nodded. "I saw."

"I'm not making this up? This is real?"

"Honey," Maya said, "it's all real."

THE DARK SIDE OF THE ROOM

Betsy cried harder, but it wasn't for herself any longer, and it wasn't because of the new resident. It was because she saw Shadow sleeping on the floor of her Memory Room, stretched out on a beautiful Oriental rug, only inches away from the wall of darkness. The black shuddered a little, and the entire wall shifted forward until it touched Shadow's paw. The gray cat's fur turned black, and the black moved up his body until he really looked like just a shadow, an outline.

"We need to tell Al," Maya said, and her voice snapped Betsy back from the Memory Room.

Betsy nodded and wiped her eyes. "He won't believe me," she said.

Maya folded her arms, brow wrinkled with concentration.

"Are there any holes in the walls, any chewed up food or nests?" she asked. "Anything at all?"

Betsy shook her head. The dead rat she'd thrown into the alley was probably gone by now. Taken by a stray cat, or even cannibalized by another rodent.

She looked around her apartment, trying to think, and her eyes came to rest on the piano, and she realized she did have proof after all.

11

The two women walked down the stairs together, and Betsy felt more uneasy with every step. Al was the last person she wanted to see about the rat problem. And she didn't need another man in her life to tell her that her problem wasn't as big as it really was. But more than that, Al gave her the willies. She avoided contact with him as much possible, going so far as to place the cash for her rent in an envelope and slide it under his door. Other residents paid online, but Betsy didn't have a computer. Couldn't see what all the fuss was about, anyway. Waste of time, she thought.

Maya kept a steady hand on her arm and talked to Betsy the whole way down.

"He'll have to do something," she said. "He can't ignore this."

Betsy snorted. "How long has the elevator been broken?"

Maya sighed, stayed quiet.

When they reached the first floor they went down the short hall that led to Al's place. Maya took Betsy's hand, gave it a squeeze, and knocked three times. Hard and confident.

They stood back and waited. When no one came, Maya knocked again, this time using a fist instead of her knuckles.

"Al," she said, making her voice bigger, "open up. We need to talk."

Betsy counted the cats she'd owned throughout her life, visualizing each one of them. She made it to sixteen (Henry) when Al opened the door. Just the sight of him made Betsy feel a little nauseous. Al was an unfortunately ugly man—slovenly, morbidly obese, with pasty, sticky looking skin, and beads of sweat dotting his forehead. His big belly pushed so far against his brown work shirt that space had opened up between the buttons, showing a glimpse of his hairy skin. He reminded Betsy of a man made of clay, poured into a mold but never shaped.

"We need you to come upstairs and take a look at something," Maya said.

Al scratched at his balding head. Flecks of dandruff dusted his shoulder. He made a show of looking at his watch.

"Unless it's a leak, it can wait 'til morning," he said. Even his voice sounded unhealthy. A throaty gurgle squeezed out through yellowing teeth.

"It can't wait," Maya said. "This needs to be addressed now."

Betsy was impressed with Maya's command, with how she didn't take no for answer and pushed back without ever raising her voice. That was real strength, Betsy thought. To be taken seriously without needing to become emotional. She imagined this was the version of Maya that worked with attorneys. People who could be different people in different circumstances always made Betsy feel envious. Because, no matter what, she always felt like herself. Like there was only one version of her, and that's all she could ever be.

"What is it?" Al said.

"Come and see for yourself," Maya said.

Al looked at his watch again, shoved one large finger up under his glasses and scratched his eye. Always scratching, Betsy thought. Every time she saw him he had an itch somewhere.

"Fine," Al said. He went back inside for a moment and came out holding a large ring full of keys and a Maglite. "If this could've waited until tomorrow—"

"Then what?" Maya said with a sharp tone. "Then what, Al?"

Al said nothing and followed them to the stairs. Betsy could hear his wheezing behind them as they climbed. At the third floor, Maya called back to him, "Kind of makes you wish the elevator worked, doesn't it?"

Al muttered a string of curses and kept going. By the time they reached the fourth floor, Betsy feared the man was going to clutch his chest and fall to the ground dead. He put both hands on his knees for a second and tried to catch his breath.

Maya walked straight to Betsy's apartment and opened the unlocked door. Betsy wasn't worried because she and Maya had already herded all the cats into the bedroom and shut the door.

"In here," Maya said.

THE DARK SIDE OF THE ROOM

Al groaned, straightened up, and went into the apartment. "What am I looking for?"

Betsy pointed at the piano.

Al shuffled over and looked at it. "I don't see anything."

"On the keys," Betsy said.

Al held up his Maglite and turned it on.

"Oh shit," he said.

Maya stood beside him. "Yes, it is," she said.

The beam illuminated at least a dozen dark brown droppings the size of sunflower seeds. Two orange-yellow stains were still drying on the white keys.

Al sighed, swung the flashlight around and inadvertently shined it right into Betsy's face. She lifted a hand to block the beam.

"A few rats, serious?" He shifted his belt to raise his pants. "Listen, ladies, this is not an emergency."

Betsy eyes burned and all she could see was white. "It's not just a few rats, Al. Ask Devin, he hears them too. There must be hundreds in the walls."

Al lowered the Maglite, hitched his pants up again, and shouldered his way past Betsy and Maya back into the hall.

"Tomorrow," he said.

Voices echoed from the staircase, and soon Greg and Jerry came into view. Jerry had his arm around his partner, head thrown back, laughing. They both stopped when they saw Al near the open door of Betsy's apartment.

"Everything okay?" Greg asked.

Betsy noticed that his fist was clenched, as if expecting a fight.

"I was just telling these ladies that I'd look into their rat problem in the morning," Al said, and his tone was different, less irritated. "Get some poison or something."

Greg's eyes narrowed and he looked to Maya, then Betsy.

Jerry stepped forward, waved his hands, "No, no. You don't want poison. They'll take it back to the nest and die there. Shit, man, they'd stink up the whole building."

Even in the lowlight, Betsy could tell Al's face had gone red.

"Well," he said, "I'll figure something out."

Jerry was nearly to the open door. He poked his head in.

"You got rats, Bets?"

She nodded.

Maya jerked her chin toward the piano. "Take a look."

Jerry went inside while Greg came over and positioned himself between Al and the two women. He towered over the superintendent, and Betsy sensed that Greg purposefully stood as tall as he could to intimidate the smaller man.

"Woo," Jerry said. "Those are some big ass rats. I've seen rat shit before, but those are some huge turds. Al, my man, you gotta deal with this."

Al's jowls jiggled as he nodded his head, "Yep, in the morning," he said. "First thing, I'll look into it."

It occurred to Betsy that they had never approached Al as a united front, asked him to address a specific problem. They'd all gone to him separately, complained about a host of issues, but never together. Was that all it took? Betsy felt a little sorry for the man, she couldn't help it. He was outnumbered, and his lack of expertise about what to do, about anything really, was painfully obvious.

Greg's low voice spoke quietly. "Why not now, Al?"

Al's fingers looped into his belt as if to pull his pants up again, but he just held them in place. He moved from one foot to the other, wouldn't look anyone in the eye for very long.

"It's late, I don't want to wake anyone up," he said.

Maya took a step closer, arms crossed over her chest. "We're all here, Al. And we just saw the new guy."

The sweat that had beaded on Al's forehead began to run down his face in shiny streaks.

"I'll call an exterminator in the morning," he said. "Promise."

Al turned to leave, stopped, and said, "Wait, new guy?"

Greg spoke up. "Why didn't you tell any of us that you rented out Campbell's old place? What with the fire and all, I thought it was damaged."

Al's mouth fell open, his small eyes creased with confusion.

"What are you talking about?" he said.

Betsy pointed down the hall. "The new resident, I met him a couple days ago."

Al looked from Greg to Jerry to Maya, like he was searching their faces for a smile, something to tell him this was a joke.

"You kidding? I haven't rented it out," he said. "My contractor friend is booked up, which is why I haven't been able to get all those other rooms fixed yet."

Betsy's heart dropped deeper inside her chest cavity. It settled somewhere beneath her lungs and made breathing difficult, shallow.

"Are you telling the truth?" Greg spoke up.

"I couldn't rent that room if I wanted to," Al said, holding up his hands. "There was a big hole in the wall from the fire."

"Sounds like you got a squatter, Al," Greg said.

Jerry leaned in the doorway. "*This* something you gonna take care of tonight?"

Once again, Betsy felt a strange pity for the man as his face got redder. She had always assumed the worst about him, but not once had she asked him how his day was going. She'd never been anything less than annoyed, and worst, down right rude. She wished she could take back all the bad thoughts she'd had about him.

With the key ring in one hand, and Maglite in the other, Al started marching down the hall.

"I'm going to take care of it right now," he said.

Betsy put out a hand, touched Al's shoulder as he walked by. He stopped.

"He's not in there," she said. "He's at Devin's."

12

Betsy closed and locked her door, then the five of them made their way down the wall to Devin's apartment.

"Drugs," Jerry whispered to Greg. "It's gotta be drugs, man."

Greg nodded, but didn't say anything. Al marched in front of the group, breathing loudly through his nose. Something warm touched Betsy's hand and her body jerked, but then she realized that Maya had taken Betsy's hand in her own and given it a light squeeze. Betsy smiled at her and gave it a squeeze back.

Al stood in front of Devin's place, and holding the Maglite under one arm, circled key after key around the ring until he found the one he wanted.

"Maybe you should knock first," Greg said.

Al looked at his keyring, and his hand was shaking, knocking the keys together with a metallic sound. His eyes looked back up to Greg and there was a pleading look there, like he had no idea what he was supposed to do next. Greg gave him a kind smile, reached over, and knocked three times on the door. The whole group leaned forward, listening for Devin's voice, for footsteps. Betsy even closed her eyes and breathed through her nose for the stench of marijuana.

There was only silence and the musty smell of the old hallway carpet.

Al lifted his keyring again, looking at Greg, but Greg lifted one finger then knocked again, harder. Still silence. He nodded and Al took the key, unlocked the door and gently pushed it open.

The door creaked and swung into a dark room. A strong odor came wafting out, something heavy and metallic. It hit the back of Betsy's throat and made her stomach churn. The others smelled it too. Maya cupped a hand over her mouth and nose, and coughed. Jerry made a disgusted noise, and Al took a step back, but Greg went right inside. The rest followed.

THE DARK SIDE OF THE ROOM

The room was exactly as it had been when Betsy had visited the other night. The same window was open with moonlight streaming in, and there was puddle on the floor, same as that night. Only this puddle didn't reflect the light in the same way. It looked darker, thicker. And the shadow on the floor next to it had shape, substance.

Greg yelled out Devin's name and ran over to the shape on the floor, fell to his knees next to it.

"Oh my god," Greg moaned.

Jerry came up beside him, said, "Holy shit. Holy fucking shit," and gagged.

There was a click as Al turned on his flashlight. "What is it?"

The beam of light moved over the floor until it came to where Greg knelt. Jerry stood a few feet away, hunched over. Greg's face had gone the color of the milk Betsy gave the cats, and his lips were a pale blue like the yarn she used to knit caps for infant boys.

Greg moved out of the way and Al's flashlight illuminated a body lying in the rectangle of moonlight that came in through the window. The head was gone, and all around that empty space was a huge, dark red puddle, mostly congealed. A few flies buzzed around and landed on the surface. The white bone of Devin's spine stood in stark contrast to the raw flesh surrounding it.

Al made a little squeak, and the flashlight beam wobbled from the body to the couch to the wall.

Betsy's skin went cold and she shivered, felt goosebumps rise up on her arms. She closed her eyes to the blood, tried to block out the smell, but it was already inside her, forming itself into an object in her Memory Room. A clear, glass vase full of dead, rotten flowers turned black and brittle. The vase full of blood.

Greg fell to his backside and put his head in both hands. Jerry come over and knelt next to him, pulled him close.

Jerry kept saying, "Shit, shit, shit."

Maya wrapped both hands around Betsy's arm and leaned close. Her fingernails dug into Betsy's skin. Maya sniffled and whispered, "Oh my god."

The room felt like it was shrinking, slowly, as if the shadows were enclosing them, but every time Betsy sensed something in her periphery and turned to look, the room, and the dark, was still. She looked back to the carnage and the dark seemed to come alive again, to be crawling along the floor and walls, spreading into the far corners of the room.

She tried to speak but could not find her voice. She stared at Devin's body.

Where was his head?

She untangled Maya's arm and took a few steps closer to the pool of blood that had spread outward from the empty neck. And it was the neck that had captured Betsy's attention. She squatted down next to Jerry and Greg, tilted her head to look closer.

"Al," she said, "can you hold the light steady?"

Al tried, but it still quivered in his shaking hand.

Greg pointed at Al, "Turn on the overheads, will you?"

Al made his way to the wall, flipped the switch, and the whole room was bathed in bright light, which brought on a new wave of moans and nausea to see Devin's headless body so clearly. His spine stuck out through torn flesh, wet and red.

"What do you see, Bets?" Jerry asked her.

She pointed one finger. "Doesn't look cut, does it?"

Greg lifted his head, looked where she was pointing. His eyes narrowed and he leaned forward, gently moved his husband's arm away.

"What do you think, a saw?" Greg asked.

Jerry's body suddenly went rigid, and he stood up quick. "Shit, man. We oughta check and make sure someone isn't still in here."

Jerry went to the kitchen, poked his head around the corner, then went in and came back out holding a steak knife. He shrugged at Maya, "It's all the dude has."

He pointed the knife at Al and said, "Come on, man. Let's go."

Al's doughy face was pale and slack. He nodded silently and followed Jerry to the single bedroom.

"Serrated knife, maybe," Betsy said, once the two men were gone. "It's uneven, and the bone looks chipped and ground up. Like it took a lot of work to get through."

Greg held his forearm to his mouth and coughed a couple times, then nodded. "The flesh too. It's not clean, that's for sure."

He stood and looked up at the ceiling, then walked around the puddle of blood and bent to look at the walls. He went over to the windows and peered at the glass.

"I'm no expert," he said, "but I don't see any blood splatter." He pointed at the couch. "There's some over there, but not what you'd expect if he got his throat cut."

THE DARK SIDE OF THE ROOM

Betsy had noticed the same thing. She, too, was no expert, but she had seen enough TV shows to know that a cut throat would send blood shooting all over the place. This all seemed low to the ground. Slow, tedious work that leaked Devin all over the floor.

Maya stepped forward, both arms wrapped around her in a self-embrace.

"When do we call the cops?" she asked.

Greg stood at the open window, his upper body leaning out into the rain. Jerry came out of the bedroom first, knife held at his side.

"No one there," he said.

Al followed close behind, flashlight clutched in both hands.

"Campbell's window is wide open," Greg said quietly.

Again, Betsy swore something moved down along the baseboards at the far end of the room. A subtle shift in the shadows where the light didn't quite reach. She motioned Al to follow her with the light, she pointed down where she'd seen the...whatever it was, and Al trained the Maglite where her finger pointed.

Al inhaled loudly. The flashlight shone on a hole

down where the floor met the wall. A hole the size of a human head and rimmed red with blood.

13

Al backed away from the hole, his mouth hanging open, and didn't stop until he bumped into the kitchen wall. The flashlight beam shrunk the farther away he got. Betsy heard him mumbling, and thought she recognized the Lord's prayer.

Jerry rattled non-stop about being in a building with an "actual fucking murderer," using the knife to punctuate each syllable, to the point that Greg put a hand on his arm and asked him to try and stay calm.

Maya took out her phone, held it close to her chest.

Betsy knelt down next to the hole, swore she heard air hissing in the space between walls.

"Al," she said, "there's nothing between this room

and Campbell's?"

The superintendent's eyes were shut tight, his mouth moving.

"Al?" Betsy said, again.

The man opened his eyes.

"No other rooms between this one and Campbell's?"

Al shook his head rapidly, closed his eyes, and resumed praying.

Betsy laid down on the floor with her head positioned so she could look directly into the bloody hole. She waved Maya over.

"Can you shine the light here?" Betsy asked.

Maya clicked her phone light on and did as she was asked. "We need to call the police, Betsy," she said, then turned to rest of the group. "We can't be playing detective right now, not with this." She pointed at Devin's corpse. "This is the real deal."

"Real fucked up," Jerry said, slashing the air with his knife. He looked at Greg, "I'm with Maya on this one. Let's get the fuck outta here and call the cops."

Betsy's cheek rested against the cold floor. She could feel the tremors and vibrations of the old building. She closed her eyes and listened, blocking out the voices behind her. There it was, that scratching. She opened her eyes and gave them a few seconds to adjust as she peered through the wall into the room beyond. Campbell's room.

An odor came drifting through, the ammonia smell of the dead rat Shadow had brought home. The dark in the room moved, shifted. A darker shade of dark. There was some faint moonlight coming between what she guessed were fluttering curtains, but the part of the room that remained in the dark seemed to move in waves, from one side to the other. Silent, slow. A chill came out through the hole, carrying a smell of blood and something else… something organic, alive.

The dark sensed Betsy, or at least she thought it did, because it stopped moving as she stared at it.

She knew it. She knew it all along.

After Robert died, she was afraid this day would come, but having Kristy was enough to keep it locked up. Once Kristy moved out and disowned her mother, it was only a matter of time before the dark that was overtaking her Memory Room broke free and flooded into the real world.

Like Maya had said, this was the real deal.

The dark was there, in Campbell's place. Growing,

waiting. It didn't want just her mind, her memories, it wanted all of her. She knew that now. It would never be satisfied until it had devoured everything inside her head, fed on all her memories of being young and in love, getting married, buying a home, raising Kristy, holding Jules, putting her granddaughter's tiny hand on a cat's fur and watching the little girl smile. Names, faces, places, dates, friends, family, jobs, TV shows and movies, books. How she felt about the world, how she loved the people in her life. All of it. The dark wanted all of her.

Up until now, Betsy had accepted her fate with quiet resignation. She knew the dark would cover her eventually. She knew where she'd end up—at the memory care facility she desperately wanted to avoid for as long as she could. Maybe, if she could accept the gradual loss of thoughts and ideas that had once seemed so important, maybe it wouldn't hurt so bad. Maybe it would be a blissful slip into the unknown. Like floating through outer space. She never dreamed that the dark would leak into the world, lash out at the people around her. People like…

Greg.

Jerry.

Maya.

THE DARK SIDE OF THE ROOM

Even Al.

And Devin.

Poor Devin.

Betsy's knees ached as she stood.

"You okay?" Maya asked.

Betsy couldn't respond. She walked past Maya with clenched fists, past Al still reciting his prayers, opened the apartment door and stepped out into the hall. She marched to Campbell's door, tried the knob, then started banging her fists against the wood.

"Open up, you coward!" She screamed. "You can't take what doesn't belong to you."

The rest of the group moved into the hall, slowly, watching as their neighbor beat against the door. Betsy kicked and hit until she was out of breath.

"You don't get to keep anyone else's head. You want what's in mine. Isn't that what you've always wanted?"

Maya had her thumbs poised over the phone to dial when Betsy rammed her shoulder into the door. She bounced backward, got a running start, and did it again. The sound reverberated deep into the room. Maya forgot about making her call and approached Betsy with one outstretched hand, like the woman was a rabid animal in need of calming.

"Hey," she said, "it's okay."

Betsy went further back, ran at the door and drove her body weight into it. There was a crack, the lock strike tore out of the frame, the door swung open and crashed into the wall, and Betsy went inside.

14

Her eyes slowly adjusted to the darkness. Moonlight glowed on one side of the room, bathing it in ghostly blue. The space was mostly bare, even more than Devin's, and what pieces of furniture remained were pushed up against the walls.

A dresser. A coffee table. An old rug lay at the very center, torn and frayed. But Betsy didn't care about the side of room illuminated by moonlight. She kept watch on the dark side, the place where all that black swirled and moved and breathed. It sensed her too. She could feel it reaching for her, wanting her, wanting to slip inside and steal whatever memories remained.

Maya came in first, saying Betsy's name, but it

caught in her throat when she saw the figure standing in the shadows.

Al came next, followed by Greg and Jerry. They all stopped when they saw it. The beam of Al's Maglite moved along the floor until it found the black shoes and pants. It moved slowly up the hem of his long, black coat, sleeves that hung low, hiding the hands, and finally up to his head. The resident stood facing the corner, rippling like he had the day Betsy first saw him. Struggling to stay upright.

A cool, musty air blew from somewhere else in the room, and it carried an awful odor rank with ammonia and death. Small lights seemed to twinkle from the far wall, thousands of them winking on and off like a city highway seen from a plane at night.

Al moved his beam and illuminated a massive hole in the wall, big enough for Greg to walk through without ducking his head, that opened up and led to the rest of the fourth floor—the part that had been burned, gutted. Betsy could still smell the charred wood, faint but present.

The resident shivered again and Al jerked the flashlight back to him. The ripples grew stronger, moving from the inside out, fluttering his long coat and pant legs, as if the man inside the clothes was turning to liquid.

Jerry said, "Oh my god," as the resident turned and took a few stumbling steps forward.

Greg spoke with a strong voice, "Stop right there. We're calling the police." He pointed a finger at the floor. "Sit down on the ground and don't move."

The resident took one more step and another ripple moved throughout his body. The upper part of the coat went slack, then the arms, the stomach and waist, until the coat was nothing more than fabric with no substance inside in. Darkness spilled out of pants, black shadows that spread outward. The clothes collapsed, like the resident had either melted, or turned into shadow. Something fell out of the hood and hit the floor with a thud. A human head rolled a few feet into the moonlight and stopped.

Maya screamed. Her phone fell out of her hand and cracked on the floor.

Devin's face stared up at the group—open mouth and empty eye sockets, the sharp nose (partially gnawed off) and pale skin covered in scratches and open sores. Al's shaking flashlight beam hit the head momentarily, and they could all see straight up into the hollowed-out skull. The white bone still covered in patches of gray.

Darkness continued to pour out of the pants, a

growing tide of inky blackness.

Jerry uttered a single, "Oh shit," as the dark wave moved toward him. Screeching and clawing, chattering their yellow teeth, were thousands of rats scurrying toward him. Jerry's hands went up to protect his face as the rats covered his feet and climbed up his legs. Within seconds Betsy couldn't see any of Jerry's clothes or skin. His entire body was a seething, undulating mass of fur and teeth and claws and tails. His screams were muffled by the rats that clung to his face, chewed his skin.

Maya turned and ran to the open door, but more rats came flooding out of the shadows and they pushed the door closed. Dozens climbed on top of others until they formed a ladder that enabled several to scurry up to the doorknob and curl around it, hissing as they did. Maya screamed again, so loud and long that her voice went hoarse. She backed away as even more rats clambered over each other until they covered the door completely.

Greg ran over and swung his arms to get the creatures off his partner, but the horde of rodents darted up his arms and swarmed his body. Jerry twitched on the floor, but Betsy couldn't tell if it was because he was still alive, or if it was the rats tugging at his skin. More came out of the shadows, an endless swell.

Greg's eyes met Betsy's, and she had never seen more fear in a human face. He yelled one word. "Run!"

Greg fell to his knees. He swiped rats off his arms and more appeared. He grabbed several and threw them across the room, but they moved too fast and his body was covered. Greg screamed and one large rat, its eyes glowing as Al pointed the flashlight to try and blind it, squirmed into Greg's open mouth. The scream turned into a choke, then into a terrible gurgling sound. Blood came pouring down his chin and soon the rat had all but vanished, except its tail that still hung out between Greg's teeth. He fell to his knees, hands scratching at his own face as rats crawled all over his head and scalp. A hole opened up in his throat, spraying blood, and a wet snout appeared, whiskers twitching. The yellow teeth bit and chewed and opened the hole further until the entire rat emerged, slick with Greg's blood.

Betsy stood perfectly still, her heart beating so hard and fast she was afraid it would it would tear lose from her arteries, come shooting out of her chest. She breathed in quick gasps, her head going light.

Al made a run for the window, screaming the whole

way. He grabbed the sill and struggled to pull himself onto the fire escape, and another wave of rats charged at him, crawled up his pants and covered his body. Others grabbed at his shoes and pants with their teeth, their claws, and dragged him back into the room. He kicked violently, screaming in higher and higher registers until his voice too, went silent, and his body went still.

Maya went down on all fours and searched blindly for her phone, but the floor was gone. From one corner of the room to the other, it was nothing but a black sea in motion with small mounds of blackness where Greg, Jerry, and Al had fallen.

And the noise, God the noise. Betsy wanted to clamp her hands over her ears, but her hands wouldn't move. Nothing would move.

Maya's hand swept along the ground, pushing aside rats only for more to move in and fill the hole.

"Please, please, please," she kept saying.

She looked over at Betsy, and her eyes went wide, her mouth opened in another scream. She flipped over onto her back, legs kicking violently, hands slapping her stomach where things moved beneath her clothes. One leg jerked and went straight, and red burst all over her white

THE DARK SIDE OF THE ROOM

blouse. Her head lolled to the side and her still open eyes stared at Betsy even as the rats began gnawing on them.

Hot tears ran down Betsy's face, her legs shook with fear. She couldn't understand why she was still alive, why they had killed everyone else but her. She looked down to see her feet, and the floor around her, completely surrounded.

The noise in the room was deafening and it made Betsy want to scream. She couldn't stop shivering, like she was standing outside in the dead of winter.

Then it stopped, all the chittering and scratching. Total silence. The dark mass of rats began to move away from her, parting as if creating a path that led from her feet to the massive hole in the wall. The rest of the room was still enveloped with black squirming bodies, thousands of them, except for this narrow pathway.

Betsy stood as still as she could, willing her body not to shake. Something was coming down the aisle the rats had created. A dark shape, low to the ground, the size of a cat. It came across the room and approached Betsy, a rat unlike anything she had ever seen or heard of. Its face twisted and contorted in ways that seemed to show intelligence, moving muscles that were dormant in all the other rats.

It came right up to her feet, its nose twitching. The rat rose up on its hind legs and sniffed at her pants. Its brow creased and its eyes narrowed. It looked up at her, held her gaze, then lowered itself and made a sound between a bark and a screech. The room immediately exploded into motion, and the rats fled the bodies, disconnected from the door, and scurried after their leader toward the hole in the wall.

Betsy waited for what seemed like minutes as every rat retreated in silence. Nothing but the sound of their claws clicking along the floor. Soon the room was emptied and Betsy was alone with the corpses of her friends and neighbors. Their bodies mangled beyond recognition. Torn apart and scattered, leaving nothing more than bones and shredded flesh.

She told her legs to move, to back up toward the door. One foot, then the other. She went slowly, humming a Phineas Priest song in her head, one played in a minor key, but she did not dare hum out loud.

This is all my fault, she thought. *The dark came out of me and found a place where it could become something real. My fault they're dead. My fault, my fault, my fault…*

THE DARK SIDE OF THE ROOM

Her back bumped into the door, she turned and opened it, stepped out into the hallway. Then, and only then, did she let out a long wail. She fell against the wall and sobbed. Blood that had splashed on her face stretched and cracked as she cried. Her sweatshirt was stained red with her friends' blood. She wiped tears away from her cheeks and felt something tickle her skin. She pulled her hand away and stared at the thin white strand stuck to her fingers.

And there, in the dim hallway light, Betsy looked down at her pants and saw they were covered in cat hair.

15

Back in her apartment, Betsy slammed the door the shut, leaned against it, and slid to the floor. She put her head down and wept as the cats gathered around her.

"Dead," she told them. "Those rats killed them all."

Starry nuzzled into her neck and purred.

Guilt pressed down on Betsy's chest like a stone and she struggled breathe. She could run, gather up the cats and take off, find another place to live. Whenever the police found the scene, they would probably assume Betsy was among the dead.

Evelyn meowed near her ear, and Betsy shook her head. No, she couldn't just leave. The dark would follow her. Or, maybe more accurately, she'd take it with her. And then this would happen again somewhere else. More people would die.

"I don't know what to do," she said.

With cats crawling all over her, Betsy closed her eyes and reopened them in the Memory Room. The dark was much closer, now. Almost all the way to the couch. So much lost inside it, she couldn't even remember all that had been forgotten. She looked down at her yellow dress, forgetting why it was this dress in particular that she chose to wear in this place.

She looked at the framed photograph of her and Robert on the wall, the two of them on the beach. Only, Betsy didn't recognize the woman in the picture. She got close and stared at the person her husband had his arm around. Young, beautiful, a bright smile, no wrinkles. And Robert, he was older than Betsy remembered. She shook her head, rubbed her eyes, and looked again. This is how Robert looked right before he died.

But he's not dead, is he?

No, not dead, even though Betsy had tried to kill his memory. He was dead to her heart, but the real Robert was still very much alive, and he had left Betsy for

THE DARK SIDE OF THE ROOM

someone else. Said he couldn't care for her any longer if she wouldn't care for herself, if she wouldn't seek the help she needed. Betsy never saw the woman he left her for, and this picture on the wall, she placed it there to remind herself of what had happened. But even that, she forgot. Instead, she imagined herself on that beach with Robert, and somewhere in the dark of her mind was the truth that this vacation had never occurred. Not with her anyway.

The room was colder now, so she went to fireplace and added a few logs to the flames. She stood in front of the warmth and watched as the fire devoured the new wood.

Betsy bit a fingernail. The flames danced, casting shadows. The heat from the fire reminded her of something. Not a memory the dark had stolen, but something she'd chosen to lock away. A rare act she had made the conscious decision to hide.

She went over to the far wall, as far away from the dark as she could get, and found a small metal chest on the ground. She tried to open it, but the lid was locked. She remembered something else, reached into her dress and pulled out a necklace, from the end of which hung a key. She put this into the lock, turned it, and opened the lid of the chest.

Inside were photographs (images of a young Betsy whispering rumors that Darcy Coleman was a slut to anyone who would listen), scraps of paper (a letter written to her by a married man she had flirted with once, he offered to leave his wife for Betsy, and to her shame she actually considered it).

The chest was full of moments like these, failures and decisions that Betsy regretted more than any others. Her fingers dug through the pile, casting aside a poker chip, a bracelet she'd stolen, a twenty dollar bill, a cassette tape, and more pieces of paper. There, at the very bottom, she found what she was looking for.

A photograph of Betsy looking very much as she did now. Her hair gray, her body carrying the extra pounds she could never seem to lose. In fact, the picture could have been taken only a few days ago.

Three months ago, Betsy thought.

She carried the photograph over to the light and stared at the image. In one hand she carried a cigarette lighter, and in the other a bottle of yellowish liquid.

"Linseed oil," she said, out loud.

She was walking down the hallway, past Campbell's place to the empty apartments. To the place where she had found the spider's nest full of cotton-white egg sacks, and thousands of tiny black bodies with all their legs, skittering up the walls and under the carpet and hiding in light fixtures. She had never planned to start such a big fire, she only wanted to get rid of them. She was finding silky webs all over her apartment, walking straight into them in the middle of the night when she woke up and had to pee. She hated the disgusting way their legs moved like each one had its own brain, the way they laid in wait for victims to trap, paralyze, and eat. So Betsy had doused the nest and egg sacks with linseed oil and set it on fire. She went back to her apartment and no one saw what she'd done. She never thought it would grow out of control and burn half the floor before the firefighters could put it out.

Linseed oil, what she had always used to clean and restore the finish on her old piano, to protect it from the humidity and the sun. The same thing her father had used when the piano sat near the living room window in her childhood home.

"Burn," Betsy said. "Burn."

She blinked twice and opened her eyes in her own apartment, sitting on the floor with the cats gathered around her.

"Burn," she said. "Those rats are going to burn in hell."

16

Betsy went into the kitchen and opened the cabinet where she kept all her cleaning supplies. Tucked behind the rags and reusable shopping bags was the brand-new one-quart bottle of linseed oil. She pulled open the junk drawer and grabbed the cigarette lighter she used for candles, then she went to the front door and paused.

There was something she needed to do, something important. She bowed her head and tried to think of what it was. It wouldn't be in the Memory Room because it wasn't yet a memory. It was something that occurred to her as she sat on the floor when she first came home.

"G flat," she yelled, and banged her forehead against the door. "What was it?"

Nothing in the world made Betsy feel more helpless as when a thought that had been so close slipped away. More often than not, she couldn't find it again. But she couldn't let that happen tonight.

What was it? What was it?

Something brushed her leg. Betsy looked down to see Starry rubbing against her, walking in slow circles, tail curling around her ankle. Betsy smiled.

She remembered.

She picked the cat up, stroked its soft black fur dotted with bits of white, and raked her fingernails through the hair until she nearly had a handful. Betsy set down the cat and wiped her hands on her chest and stomach. Bits of fur clung to the still sticky blood on her sweatshirt. She went over to the scratching posts and cat towers, and gathered as much hair as she could find. Fistfuls of gray, white, orange, and black. Betsy ran the fibers through her hair, ran fur covered fingers along her pant legs until her clothes looked like some kind of ridiculous costume.

All five of the cats were gathered, staring at her with watchful eyes. Sensing, she thought, that something bad had happened.

"I have to go," she told them. "You all saw what

happened to Shadow, and I need to make sure that doesn't happen to any of you."

Shasta padded closer, meowed.

"I don't know if I'll be back," Betsy said, scratching the cat's head. "There's a lot of them and only one of me."

She picked up Shasta, held the animal close, felt its purr like a warm shiver.

"Look out for Starry," Betsy said, "and make sure Topsy and Turvy eat enough. You can afford to lose some weight, but they're still so small."

Betsy carried the cat over to the window, gave it a kiss on the head, and gently set it down on the fire escape. The other cats had followed, and she picked them up, one by one, said their names, and put them outside.

Starry was last. Such a beautiful, inquisitive creature.

Betsy rubbed behind Starry's ears and he pushed into her hand, eyes closed.

"I'll miss you most," Betsy said. "You were there for me when no one else was. Something bad is going to happen and we all need to leave. I need you to get the others somewhere safe, okay?"

Starry looked at her, and Betsy thought he

understood. She gave him one last squeeze, then placed him on the fire escape. She grabbed the flashlight, linseed oil, and cigarette lighter off the counter. Tears burned her eyes as she looked at all the animals she loved so much.

"Take care of each other," she said. "I hope to see you soon."

Evelyn jumped up on the window sill, then down to the floor. Topsy, Turvy, Shasta, and finally Starry, all did the same.

"No," Betsy said, raising her voice. "You have to go. It isn't safe here."

She tried to shoo them back out the window, but the cats scattered, ran to hiding spots throughout the apartment. Only Starry remained, watching his owner with a tilted head and curious eyes. Betsy fought tears as she said, "Please, get them out. Promise me."

Starry blinked once, and Betsy took that as a "yes."

As soon as she left the apartment and looked at the objects she carried, Betsy Lupino's tears stopped. For now, the dark was on one side of the hallway, and she was determined not to let it get any closer.

17

The door to Campbell's old apartment didn't close all the way because of the broken strike. It was cracked open just enough to the see one chewed up high heel, and one skeletal foot, covered only with thin strips of red flesh.

Maya.

Betsy shouldered the door open more and went inside. She kept the flashlight off and told herself not to look, not to look, not to look…

But the bodies were unavoidable. If she hadn't known them when they were alive, there was no way Betsy could have identified these people. She doubted their own families would be able to tell who they were.

Greg's ribcage was opened up and emptied, and

the hole in his throat was still visible. His eyes were gone and his teeth were stained with blood that looked black in the moonlight.

She couldn't stand the sight of Al, or what was left of him. His body looked like there had been a bomb inside his stomach. He was blown apart, scattered. Betsy tiptoed through pieces of his meat, felt the softness of it under her shoes. She gagged and tasted stomach acid.

A ringing broke the silence, startling Betsy so much she nearly dropped the flashlight, and a blue light glowed on floor near the wreckage of Maya's body. Betsy went over and saw the dead woman's cell phone, lying in a pool of blood. She picked it up with two fingers, holding it carefully, and pushed the answer button.

"Hello?" Betsy said.

"Ma'am," a woman's voice said, "this is 911 dispatch, we received a call from this number that got disconnected. I want to confirm that you are okay."

Betsy turned the flashlight off so she wouldn't have to look at all the damage surrounding her.

"Ma'am," the voice said, "are you okay?"

Betsy shook her head, the fingers holding the phone sticky with Maya's blood.

THE DARK SIDE OF THE ROOM

"No, I'm not," she said. "But I will be."

She hung up the phone, and gently set it back down on the floor. Standing in this room of death, Betsy wanted to say something, felt like she *should* say something, but she didn't have the words. Her head was a creaky machine, and the gears were grinding together, producing thoughts and images that didn't even make sense most of the time. Her hands shook and her knees were weak with fear, but she had to keep going before this plan, such as it was, got covered up in the dark.

At the far side of the room, she clicked the flashlight on and before her was the massive hole in the wall. The sheetrock had small, ragged edges. Chewed open, it looked like. The smell was so much stronger than she remembered. A horrible combination of burned wood, ammonia, and the warm odor of living things huddled together in filth.

Betsy shined the light into the hole in the wall and walked inside. She saw all the way through one apartment and to the charred remnants of the one beyond that. The walls separating units had been mostly torn down after all the water damage, so the apartments connected as though they were one large room. Even the walls between apartments and hallway had been mostly burned, so the space was a massive echoing chamber of blackened wood and moving shadows. Al's contractor friend had come and put in support beams, so every twenty feet or so there was a fresh piece of lumber. Out of place in all the other torched wood. All of the windows had been painted black from the inside, and covered with tarps on the outside, so no light came through at all.

Betsy went deeper into the space, listening for movement, for chattering teeth and scratching claws. She heard a few small squeaks as she passed the skeleton of a kitchen. The sink had fallen through to the floor and sat there lopsided.

Deeper and deeper she went until Betsy couldn't even see the hole she'd come through when she turned around. She didn't see any spiderwebs, though, and for that she was grateful.

Those squeaks she heard multiplied the farther she walked, until there seemed to be hundreds of them, coming from all around her. Claws clicked on the floors, scampered across the rafters. She was being followed, watched. There was something up ahead, and the noises she heard were the scouts—investigating, reporting back on her position. She knew it. She could sense their alertness, their agitation.

THE DARK SIDE OF THE ROOM

And from somewhere back there, in the dark, she felt a sort of pressure, a change in the air, as if the molecules were vibrating in a different way.

Her shoes crunched over something on the ground. Each footstep louder than the last. She shined the light down and saw thousands, if not millions, of rat turds. The entire floor was black with the small bits of feces, and each step unleashed a wave of foul, organic odor. Betsy tried breathing through her mouth, but she could taste the dust of the turds and that made her stomach boil. Smelling it was the lesser of two evils, so she breathed through her nose again and trudged on.

The squeaks got louder, more frantic, as Betsy continued. Her skin crawled at the sound of them scurrying around her, invisible. Sometimes she saw bright pinpoints glowing in the darkness, winking on and off. Eyes watching her. Dust drifted down into her hair as something scratched along the rafters. She jerked the flashlight up, but it was already gone. Something else darted past her legs, close enough to feel its movement. She clutched the bottle of linseed oil close and kept going.

She kept the flashlight pointed ahead, following the weak path it created in the darkness that surrounded her.

Her foot kicked something on the ground, something solid that rolled out of the way. Betsy moved the beam and illuminated a human head, empty eye sockets and open mouth. The hair looked brittle and covered in dust. Where the neck would be was wide open, like Devin's head. She took a step closer and caught a whiff of rotting meat, saw movement inside the mask. Small white worms, squirming around the bone of the skull, spilling out what was left of the nose.

Betsy gagged and moved the beam away so she couldn't see the head any longer. Her arms and hands went weak, and the flashlight shook back and forth. She grabbed a handful of sweatshirt and pulled it up over her mouth and nose.

The face, such as it was, had been familiar. It was the face she saw when she first met the new resident. It used that head until it couldn't any longer, then it took Devin's and used that.

Betsy gag reflex triggered again, so she moved away, blinking back the tears that burned her eyes.

The squeaks turned into screeching as Betsy went through the burned remains of the last apartment on the floor. She knew it was the last because the end units were bigger, had a different layout than the others. The sound of the rats made her think of what Devin had said about the rain. That felt like months ago, and Betsy was surprised she remembered his words at all. What had he called it? A symphony? The rats' screeching was a symphony too. A dark symphony of angry, violent sounds. Teeth and claws and shivering throats.

They're sounding the alarm, Betsy thought. *Too late for that.*

She stepped over the shattered tile of a bathroom floor, narrowly avoided banging her skin into a cracked bathtub. To her left, she saw a pile of broken things—large and small, curved and straight. She got closer and sucked in a breath, felt her chest go tight when she noticed the teeth on the floor. Hundreds of bones picked clean and scattered. Some clearly from small mammals, and others big enough to be human. Dust drifted into her nostrils and she stifled a cough by holding an arm against her mouth.

Something caught the light and glinted within all the bones. Betsy knelt down and moved away some of the pieces. Her heart turned into a hammering, quivering thing as she picked up a shredded blue collar, stained with blood. A silver circle hung off it, engraved with the word

"Shadow."

It took everything Betsy had not to scream. Instead, her pain came out in a low growl, like an animal, and she wrapped her fingers around the tag so tight she felt it digging into her skin.

The rats' screeching stopped all at once. It didn't die down or grow quiet. It was there one second, and gone the next.

Betsy froze and turned off the flashlight. She listened. There was another sound in the space, a sound that made the back of her knees go numb. It came from up ahead, near where she knew the very back wall of the Parkrose apartment complex would be.

A moist, sucking sound, like someone squeezing handfuls of wet mud until it came oozing out between their fingers. Teeth chittering, fast purring. There was an occasional squeal, but mostly it was the sound of movement, of something large.

Betsy tiptoed forward and unscrewed the cap of the linseed oil, caught a whiff of the sweet, grainy liquid inside. She held the oil in one hand and reached into her pocket with the other, took out the cigarette lighter, then turned on the flashlight.

THE DARK SIDE OF THE ROOM

Her mind couldn't find words. Her mouth went dry.

The dark wave that had spilled throughout Campbell's old apartment and devoured her friends, it was collected here against the far wall. A rolling, seething horde of rats. With so many of them, it was hard to make out the individual creatures, they were combined into one shapeless, black mass that rose nearly to the ceiling.

The black shape rose and fell, as if it were breathing. They were silent except for the slick wetness of their bodies slithering over and under each other in unison. Hundreds of pairs of eyes watched her, disappeared into the writhing wave, and others emerged, their pinhead eyes reflecting the light.

Betsy took a breath, wanted to scream with all her strength at this creature (because she thought of it not as a group, but as one mind), but her shallow breathing and weak legs made it hard to speak.

"You can't take anymore," she whispered.

At the sound of her voice, the black wave started writhing faster. Betsy thought of thick oil, of boiling liquid. Rats from the outer edges moved inward, collecting at the center until the mass took on a gigantic oval shape. Near the top, two dark cavities appeared as some of the rats fell inward, were reabsorbed into another place, and those cavities looked like eyes. Dead, black eyes.

The rats churned at the bottom of the oval, creating a line that looked like a lipless mouth.

Betsy could barely stand. Her pulse quivered in her neck erratically as she looked at this giant face. A larger rat appeared at the very top and sat there like a crown on the head. The same rat that had approached her in Campbell's apartment, the one whose face seemed to contain intelligence. They stared at each other and the rat's head tilted. Its eyes narrowed. It made a sound like a bark and the mouth of the giant face split open into an even larger cavity, and Betsy stared into a tunnel of swirling rats.

The tunnel pulled in air as thousands of rats breathed together, and it made a sound that Betsy understood as a word.

Here.

Air rushed out of the throat, rancid and warm, and she heard, *Now.*

Again.

Here.

Now.

THE DARK SIDE OF THE ROOM

Betsy swallowed hard and looked straight at the rat king on top of the face.

"I am here now," she said, and when the mouth opened again, Betsy rushed forward and squeezed the bottle of linseed oil. Liquid shot out, into the throat. The quiet was instantly shattered by squeals and chittering. The face began to melt, to lose shape, as the rats moved frantically over each other.

Betsy squeezed the bottle until it was almost empty, then poured what was left on the ground. She knelt and flicked the cigarette lighter to a flame, and touched it to the oil. Fire tore across the floor and into the still open mouth of the churning face. Light burst in bright holes in the cheeks, the forehead. The squealing turned into shrieks as the rats caught fire.

Betsy backed away as the face lost all shape and collapsed. The king fell somewhere into the mass, his bark rising above all the shrieking and chittering. Silver smoke rose up and rolled along the ceiling, carrying the smell of burnt flesh and fur. Betsy coughed and her eyes burned.

She wouldn't lock this memory away. This fire she wanted, needed to remember.

Small black bodies ran out of the mass, engulfed in

flames, screaming high pitched screams, only to shudder, fall over, and go silent. One crawled toward her, its front claws dragging itself, its back legs shriveled and useless. Betsy stood over the creature, lifted her foot, and smashed it down on the rodent's head. She felt the small crack of its skull, and blood leaked out from under her shoe.

The smoke was getting thicker, filling the room. The ceiling was now on fire, and flames crept along the floorboards. Betsy knew, if she didn't leave now she might not ever get out. The shrieking was so loud that her ears ached. A piercing sound that clenched her teeth together. She was about to turn and run back to Campbell's when she saw the mass of rats separating. Those on fire were moved, or pushed, to one side of the room, and those that were not rolled to the other side, still moving in unison.

In the orange glow of the flames, Betsy saw the king open his mouth, and this smaller group of rats turned their heads in unison until all of their eyes stared directly at her. Betsy turned and ran as the rats spilled forward and rushed after her.

The shrieking died down as the fire consumed half of the group, and now she could hear the chattering teeth and hoarse squeaks coming up behind her. If she could just make it to the hall, get to her own apartment and make sure all the cats got out safely…if she could save something at the end of all this, maybe then she could rest.

She took a quick glance over her shoulder and saw hundreds of rats, some running, some climbing up each other to form a long extension of claws and teeth. Reaching for her.

Betsy pumped her arms and legs, ran faster. Her foot stepped on something that rolled and there was a sharp snap in her ankle. She cried out and fell to the ground. She opened her eyes and found herself staring into the empty eyes of the rotted human head.

She screamed and kicked as the rats flooded around her feet, her broken ankle. Their teeth tore at her shoes, her socks. She kicked, connected with a small group that scattered, then collected again and attacked. Pain shot up her legs as hundreds of teeth bit into her toes. Her nerves carried ice as her flesh was opened.

Smoke filled her lungs. Her vision went blurry. More rats scurried up her body, and the last thing she saw before she closed her eyes was the King sitting on her chest, looking down into her face as flames rose up behind him.

The fire grew and Betsy closed her eyes. She went

to the Memory Room and the dark was no longer there. The whole room was bathed in the beautiful orange-red light of a sunset, and she saw all those memories and objects that had been hidden for so long. She smiled and felt the warmth of the light on her face.

MAJOR / MINOR

From *The Oregonian*

Woman found injured on the 4th floor of the Parkrose apartment complex after a 3rd floor neighbor called the fire department. The bodies of five other residents were found dismembered in a section of the building damaged by an earlier fire 3 months prior. Police suspect that the deceased may be the latest victims of the killer who has been targeting the homeless population.

The woman was transferred to the hospital where she is currently undergoing surgery.

Rain tapped against the window, pulling Betsy from sleep. The curtains were open and she could see the dark clouds outside, the trees swaying in the wind. Her head was foggy from all the meds, but the doctor told her she'd be able to stop taking them once the pain was a little better.

She grabbed the control and pushed the button that lifted the head of her bed. Now she could see the flat space under the blanket where her right leg should have been. They were able to save the left foot, although she lost a couple toes, but the right was too far gone. Just below the thigh, there was nothing. The stump was still wrapped in bandages, and occasionally the pain was so intense that it cut through the morphine they gave her to sleep, and that pain felt like teeth gnawing at her bone all over again.

When she had first awakened here and saw the IV in her arm, the paper-thin gown draped over her body, she thought she was in the hospital. Over the last couple of days, though, Betsy had seen enough people, patients she supposed, shuffling by her open door, wearing their own clothes. And the room itself was half apartment, half hospital suite. And the way the staff spoke to her like she was child, the flashcards they held up and asked her to remember later, all told her she had ended up in the one place she'd been trying to avoid all this time.

It was bound to happen eventually, but Betsy still hated the helpless feeling it gave her. She imagined the medications they gave her would only make her more compliant, less herself, so she took to hiding them under her tongue until the nurse started asking Betsy to open her mouth. After that, Betsy waited until the nurse left the room and made herself throw up into the trashcan next to her bed. She'd then cover the bile covered pills in wrinkled up tissue paper.

Except the morphine, she took that pill because she couldn't think through the pain otherwise.

Betsy stared out the window at the storm, heard the distant concussion of thunder. She checked the Memory Room at least once day, had actually made some adjustments to it. The dark had retreated back toward the far wall, but it was still there, still breathing. She had put a cork board near the fireplace and hung up a few pictures.

A dark shape moved along the window sill. Betsy held her breath as it jumped to the floor, came over and climbed up onto her bed. She exhaled when she saw Starry's sweet face, heard the comforting rhythm of his purring.

THE DARK SIDE OF THE ROOM

Betsy pulled the cat closer and stroked its soft fur. Starry was the only cat they found after the fire had been put out. Betsy's heart ached to think of what had happened to all the others, but she had to believe they were out there, somewhere, looking after each other, keeping safe and warm. But Starry, he had stayed behind, knowing he'd find his way to Betsy eventually, and he did.

Starry curled on Betsy's stomach and put his mouth to his paws, started eating something that made an awful crunching sound.

"What is that?" Betsy asked.

Starry looked up at her with a blank expression, a long, thin piece hanging out of his mouth.

Betsy took it, held it up to the light. Brown, with small, stiff hairs sticking out. A leg, it looked like. She gently moved Starry's paws away from the thing he'd been eating, and Betsy nearly vomited. A sleek body, shiny and black, broken apart by Starry's teeth. Yellow guts were spilled out on Betsy's gown. There was no mistaking that shield-shaped body and long antennae. One crooked wing still twitched.

"Where did you find this?" Betsy asked the cat.

Starry turned back to his catch and started eating

again. Betsy's stomach clenched and she shooed the cat away.

Betsy muttered, "E-sharp," and stripped off the gown, threw it across the room. She pulled the thin blankets up to her chin and let the morphine carry her back to sleep.

She woke up to a sound she thought at first was birds, but when she opened her eyes and looked out the window it was still dark and raining. A chirping sound, almost musical, came from behind her head. Betsy turned, as much as she could, and heard it again, not in the room, though, in the wall. Not just one chirp, but many of them, dozens even, all going at once.

Betsy sat upright, leaned her head against the wall, and heard scratching—the sound of hundreds of legs scurrying in the walls, digging at the insulation. Her heart sank down to her stomach and settled there.

She closed her eyes and entered the Memory Room. Tears burned her eyes as she looked at the wall of darkness. It had moved forward once again and covered all those memories that were briefly hers. Thankfully, the photograph on the wall of her and Robert on that beach (Mexico, was it?) was still in the light. She couldn't remember any of the specifics of that trip—even the dress she wore was unfamiliar—but it looked beautiful. How she wanted to be back there, in the sun, in the light.

Betsy went over to the cork board and looked at the pictures she'd pinned there.

Photographs that would remind her she had fought the dark before, and she could do it again.

ALONG the SHADOW

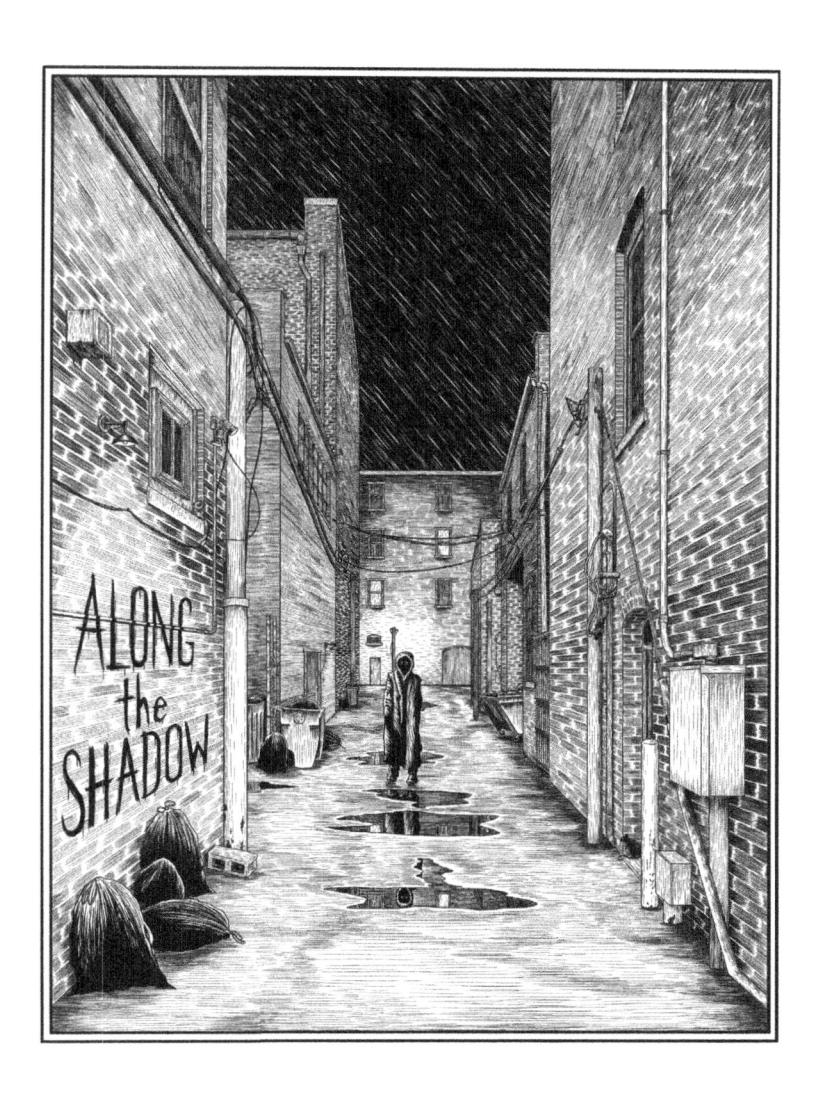

1

Gary Shaw woke up, not to an alarm, but his cell phone ringing. His eyes scanned the room slowly and looked at the window. The curtains were open, and it was still dark outside, which was not a good sign.

He rubbed his aching eyes with one hand while the other hand blindly searched the nightstand for his phone. He found it, squinted in the glow of the screen, and answered it.

"Shaw," he said.

He listened to the voice on the other end, sighed, and said, "Another one? I thought those were Coleman's?"

He listened some more.

"Okay, okay. Give me ten minutes," he said, then

hung up.

Shaw lay in the dark, listening to the rain rush down the gutters of the apartment building. His head still felt a little heavy from the wine and cigarettes, but he knew there was no way he'd be falling back to sleep tonight.

He groaned out of bed, stumbled across the room to the chair where he'd thrown his clothes. Same clothes he'd worn the day before. Like anyone would care. They'd be soaked in minutes anyway once he went outside.

His partner, Roberto Villanueva, always told him to get a hat, a fedora like they wear in the movies. Shaw said that was the last thing he wanted, to look like a cop from a movie. It was bad enough the stares, the threats and insults, the spitting when people figured you for a cop. Wouldn't do any good to go around looking like one.

Lately, it had gotten so bad Shaw had started telling people, "I'm not a fucking cop. I'm a detective."

And not just a detective, a homicide detective. The job every beat cop wants until they're knee-deep in blood, and brain matter, and shit. Yes, shit. That's something they don't tell you right away. A dead body always defecates once it expires. Always.

The movies don't show that.

ALONG THE SHADOW

Shaw slipped on his pants and shirt, started to tuck it in, decided against it, and threw on a sweater. The nights were getting colder. Days, too, for that matter. His boots were still damp from the day before, and they were only going to get wet again. He pulled on a raincoat, grabbed his badge, gun, and wallet from the dresser. He headed for the front door and stopped when he saw his telescope in the living room, pointed at the glass of a rain-splattered window. It was an old one, beat up and scarred. The same one he bought in high school, back when he thought he might want to be an astrophysicist, back when the world seemed endless and bright. He knew now the world was finite and ugly, but the universe…the universe was all beauty and fire and light. Over the years, he had replaced a few pieces—the finderscope, the lens, the eyepiece—but most of it was still original. Like it mattered. It was a cheap telescope, even back when he bought it, but it became something of an addiction when he began to spot planets, stars, galaxies, all from his childhood bedroom.

He went over to the window, opened it, and wished he had a place in the country. Somewhere far from all the light pollution of the city. He leaned over and looked through the eyepiece, turned the focusing knob until he saw a few pinpoint lights in the black canvas of space. Tiny dots of white, sending their light across the vast reaches of space. To see those lights was to see the universe as it was millions of years ago. When he was young, he wondered if he could point the telescope in the other direction and see the future. See where all the light was going. And that was something else Gary Shaw learned. You can see the past clearly, but the future is always in the dark.

He closed the window, went out into the hall, locked the door behind him, and went downstairs.

Once Shaw stepped outside into the rain, he turned and gave the brick apartment building the middle finger. It was a ritual of his ever since he moved in five months earlier. Anne had taken almost everything in the divorce. He had never cheated on her, hit her, and he had only ever screamed at her once. Still, just being married to him somehow entitled her to everything he had worked so hard to obtain. The house. The furniture. His money. Not to mention sole custody of their two boys. He had no idea what they'd said when the child psychologist spoke to them, but he could guess it was more Anne's words than their own that came out of their mouths. She always had a way of speaking through them. Of getting them to say the things that she was too cowardly to say herself.

Still, he loved her. He'd be lying if he said he didn't. The divorce was a surprise, the worst kind, and you don't just go turning off love like a switch. He was still hurt, maybe even bitter, but part of that was because he missed her. And maybe that was his fault. He only remembered the good times. What were they? Moments, hours, days, years? When things had got bad, and he went quiet, when Anne stopped asking him questions and stared at him with a hurt expression, he somehow blocked those times out. He thought they were those down days you expected to have, but maybe they stretched out and turned into the way it always was. But he wasn't sure. He never could trust his memory, not when it came to his home life. At a crime scene, nothing escaped him. And maybe that's what the marriage was now. A death. A chalk outline of something that used to be alive.

A miserable Portland night. Cold, wet, and dark. The kind of night where you couldn't even light a cigarette. It was so wet. Shaw still felt the heaviness of the wine in his head. Made the world shudder to move into frame whenever he turned to look at something, so he decided to walk. He could make it where he was going as fast as he could driving anyway. He pulled the hood of his jacket up over his head and trudged through the night.

Halloween was only a week away, and he saw the glowing triangle eyes of jack 'o' lanterns in some of the apartment windows. It made his heart ache that he had no idea what his kids would dress up as this year. Or if they even wanted to dress up. With the way Anne was raising them now, they'd probably just want to stay inside and watch stupid videos on the internet, play video games.

Rain fell through the haloes of lampposts and the yellow, red, and green of traffic lights. Cars sent sprays of water onto the sidewalk as they drove past. A few bars were still open. A few stragglers leaned over a half-finished pint.

Shaw passed a doorway, a brick arch in the building, and saw a dark mound on the ground. As he got closer, the mound moved, shifted, and let out a cough. Someone stood across the street, facing him, standing there motionless.

Every once in a while, Shaw saw the city through the eyes of someone who didn't live here, grow up here. And in those moments, he saw it as something ominous, foreboding. A place he'd never want to be. It wasn't always this way. Years ago, it was a place for bands to be discovered, for films to be made. A place of art and creativity and weirdness. There were still bumper stickers that said, "Keep Portland Weird." But it wasn't weird anymore. There was something darker than that here now, and he wasn't sure when it all changed. The homeless, the addicts, they never used to bother him. They were harmless at best. Most fell off the I-5 at some point on their way to a better life, and here they landed.

Now, though. Everyone on the streets seemed hostile, distrusting. He wasn't exactly afraid, but he wasn't at ease either.

Shaw crossed 11th Street and took a left on Everett. It wasn't long before he made it to the Park Blocks. A few tents were set up in the grass, shopping carts parked outside, piled high with God-knew-what, and covered with tarps. A person lay curled on a bench, tucked into a sleeping bag.

Voices shouted. Slurred, angry, and Shaw turned to see two men stumbling through the park. They spoke at the same time, over each other, but Shaw couldn't understand a word of what they were saying. They lurched on, down the low-lit streets of trash-filled gutters and boarded up stores. There were a lot of more those these days, too. So many windows and doors covered in plywood, then later spray painted by some graffiti artists. You could walk blocks without ever seeing your reflection.

A few more blocks, and Shaw saw the red and blue lights flashing up ahead. The structures started at Broadway, but grew bigger, more connected a few blocks down. Structures built by the homeless who decided to camp together. They'd collect whatever materials they could find and fit them into something resembling a shelter. More people would join in, and soon these structures would cover the sidewalk of an entire block.

A city within the city.

Shaw couldn't think of them as camps, because to look at the outside you weren't sure what they were. Cardboard, trash bags, buckets, pieces of wood, tarps, blankets, plastic from construction sites, traffic cones, stolen bikes, baby strollers, old screen doors. All of it assembled into something that looked more like an abstract art exhibit than any kind of shelter.

Three cop cars blocked off the street to through-traffic, and an unmarked car sat parked on the opposite side. Robby's car.

As he got closer, Shaw saw Robby standing over a man sitting on the curb in front of the chaotic collection of debris that made up the homeless encampment. Not far from them was a mound on the street. A mound not unlike the one Shaw had passed in the doorway earlier.

Shaw showed his badge to the patrolmen standing outside the cars, the strobes from the lightbars casting carnival colors over the shelter. A pair of eyes peeked out at him from between torn pieces of fabric, then disappeared.

Robby stood up straighter as Shaw approached.

"I told you to drive," Robby said.

"Ten minutes," Shaw said. "Same amount of time."

"Fuck you, it was twenty-two minutes, and my new friend here doesn't want to say much." Robby tapped his shoe against the foot of the man, sitting with both hands on his head. "Do you?"

The man looked up, startled, and the face was a lot younger than Shaw expected. Mid-twenties, maybe, but the drugs and elements had weathered his skin so that it looked much older. But the eyes were still young, barely.

Robby put a hand on Shaw's back and led him away. "Think real hard about what you saw," he called back to the young man.

"What are we doing here, Robby?" Shaw said. "This should be Coleman's case."

Robby leaned in and lowered his voice., "They can't find him, not even his wife knows where he is."

"He got someone on the side?"

"Coleman? No way, man. He's devoted to the missus."

"He a drinker?"

Robby looked over at the officers standing watch near the encampment. "I heard the dudes talking. They say Coleman is missing."

"Missing?"

"Never came home from the last murder, couple days ago. The body went to the morgue, and Coleman stayed behind to search the scene. From there," Robby snapped his fingers, "gone. Had to tow his car back to the station."

"Shit."

"Shit is right, which is why we're here. When your varsity players go AWOL, you call in the JV squad."

"What is this, the third one?" Shaw asked.

"Fourth," Robby said. "Seems to fit with the others."

They neared the covered mound on the street, and Shaw could already smell the blood. That liquid, metallic odor, and the shit too. He smelled that immediately.

"You alright?" Robby asked.

Shaw sighed, reached for his pack of cigarettes, and realized he'd forgotten to grab them. Which was for the best because ever since the divorce, Robby would not stop hounding him about his health—physical and mental—and then he'd get good and pissed whenever Shaw didn't want to hear it.

"Fine," Shaw said. "Tired."

"Yeah, yeah," Robby said. "And you smell like wine. A little hungover, perhaps? Hmm?"

"Not hungover yet," Shaw said. "Still drunk. Tell me about our ghost."

"Show, then tell," Robby said. He bent down, grabbed the cloth, and gently pulled it back.

Whatever Shaw had been expecting, it wasn't this. The body of an adult man, lying face down on the street. Except it wasn't really face down because there was no face. There was nothing but a bloody stump where the head should have been.

"No I.D., no wallet, no keys," Robby said. "His clothes look like they haven't been washed in a fucking year, and his shoes are worn down to nothing. He's probably one of them," nodding to the encampment, "but pendejo over there won't say anything. We don't know who called it in. My guess is el pendejo. They probably have at least one cell phone in that pile of shit. We tried calling back but got no answer."

Shaw got on his knees and looked at the empty neck, the torn flesh where the head should have been. He looked up to the sky, saw each and every raindrop falling through the streetlamp halo.

"No sign of the head?" Shaw asked. "No blood trails?"

Robby tapped his foot in the water. "If there were, they've washed away."

A small portion of the spine stuck out of the bloody flesh. A dark puddle had gathered all around the body and ran in a small river toward the storm drain near where the young man sat, cradling his head in both hands again.

"It's not clean," Shaw said.

"I noticed that."

"I mean, it doesn't look like a knife, does it?"

Robby knelt next to him and pointed at a flap of skin near the windpipe.

"It's jagged there, so it could be a knife. Serrated,

maybe, but not like a nice one from a hunting store. More like a steak knife."

Shaw nodded. He was right. Small ripped edges of cartilage and muscle that reminded him of something he couldn't quite place. Maybe steak is exactly what he was thinking of. Bloody steak cut with a cheap blade.

Shaw wiggled his fingers in the air and waited until Robby took a pair of surgical gloves from his coat pocket and handed them over. Shaw pulled each one on with a snap, then grabbed the man's shirt and rolled the body so that it laid on its back. He pulled up the shirt to expose the man's stomach and chest. The blood had pooled along the length of the torso, giving the skin the reddish-purple tint of a bruise.

"Liver mortis," Shaw said. "So, we're talking two to three hours."

Robby took out a small notepad and covered it with a hand to keep the rain from hitting it.

"Which means pendejo waited at least an hour before calling."

"Unless he didn't see anything," Shaw said.

"Oh, he saw something. Look at him. He's not mute just because he saw a dead guy."

Shaw closed his eyes and ran his gloved hands over the victim's torso, feeling for anything unusual—a small depression where the blade of a knife had slipped in and punctured the heart, a lung. Once he was satisfied there was nothing, he rolled the body again and searched the back. Nothing.

Robby groaned and popped his back, looked over at the man on the sidewalk.

"Since your twenty-two-minute walk caused you to miss out on my extensive interrogation, allow me to fill you in. Pendejo over there hasn't said a word. What you see now is how he's been since we arrived. Just sitting there like an asshole and holding his head like it's about to fall off. So, with my unparalleled powers of observation, I suspect that the murderer belongs to this tribe of nomads known as the homeless. And this is why pendejo is scared. If he says anything, he could be next. Following me so far?"

Shaw nodded, but he wasn't listening. He had seen so many murder victims over the years that the violence didn't even shock him anymore. He saw it, smelled it, felt the intensity of it, but it didn't shake him like it used to. It was more clinical now. And the first thing he looked for when he was called to a fresh one was the cause of death. Nine times out of ten, it was obvious. Gunshot wound. Stabbing. Strangulation. The foaming mouth of an overdose. A brick to the face. A broken neck. He'd seen it all. But this was the first decapitation he had come across, and he didn't like that the cause of death wasn't clear. Without the head, he couldn't know if the victim had taken a bullet to the brain or a screwdriver up the nose. And if Shaw had to guess, the man was killed somehow before his head was sawed off.

"I woke up everyone inside that…thing," Robby said, pointing to the encampment, "and dragged their asses out here. All of them had been sleeping or claimed they were. A few were doing the 'ol inebriation shuffle and mumbling nonsense. No one had anything to tell me, and they were all genuinely shocked to see the body. All except for our friend pendejo."

Shaw grabbed one of the victim's hands and unrolled the fingers. Small open sores, fresh and bloody, dotted the skin. One fingertip was completely raw like it had been scraped along the asphalt. The wounds were too big to be track marks, and there were too many of them. Dozens, if not more.

Shaw reached up and gently ran his fingers along the exposed bone of the spine. Tiny grooves and scratches caught the glove. Definitely a serrated blade, but the killer didn't have a strong knife, just like Robby said. It must have taken a lot of patience to make it all the way through that bone.

2

Shaw covered the body back up and stood. He turned his face to the sky and let the cool water fall on his skin. His stomach clenched and went sour. Somewhere out there in the city was this man's severed head. Not only that, someone most likely had in their possession. Maybe it was on a shelf in a freezer with snowflakes forming on the eyelashes, gray eyes frozen in a lifeless stare whenever the killer opened the door. Or maybe it had been disposed of in a dumpster, a park, or thrown in the Willamette River. Either way, it was out there, and someone with blood-covered hands was alive and breathing in the city.

"We should have some officers search the area for the head," Shaw said, without looking at Robby. "Check trash cans, dumpsters, parks."

"On it," Robby nodded. He jogged over to the cops standing near the cars and started talking to them.

Shaw felt the gentle pressure of raindrops tapping on his skin, running into his hair and down his neck. He felt something else on his neck, too. A pressure, a feeling of being watched. He turned quickly and found himself staring at the brick wall of a building, a few high windows, all dark. He thought he saw something move in the shadows along the sidewalk—small white dots, like the stars through his telescope—but the longer he watched, he realized it was just water flowing into the drain.

He turned and looked back at the man sitting on the curb. He had lifted his head and was looking right at Shaw, now. Robby was busy pointing and giving directions, so Shaw walked over and sat on the curb next to the man. The man blinked hard and stared straight ahead.

Shaw put his hands in his pockets and felt something. He pulled out a single cigarette, snapped in half. He tore off the filter, licked his fingers, and twisted the paper together. He took out his lighter, lit the cigarette, and blew the smoke into the sky.

"When you see something like that," he said,

pointing with the two fingers that held the cigarette, "your mind isn't sure what to do with it, you know? It's brutal, it's bloody, and it doesn't make sense. At least not right away. After a few days go by, you start to remember these little details that you blocked out. A sound, maybe. Like how his screaming turned into gurgling as he drowned in his blood. A sound like that, you don't ever forget it. Not really."

Shaw looked at the side of the man's face, at his widened eyes.

"You know the sound I'm talking about?"

The man's eyes closed, his head lowered, and he nodded once.

"Hey, that's good. Tell you what? I'm going to ask a few questions, okay? You don't have to say a word. You just nod or shake your head. That way, anyone asks if you talked, you can say 'no' and mean it. Sound like a plan?"

The man sighed, rubbed his fingers together, and nodded again.

"Good," Shaw said. "Do you live here?"

A nod.

"Did you see him die?"

Not a nod, but not a shake. A sort of back and forth.

"Not the whole thing? Part of it?"

A nod.

"The end?"

A slow nod.

Shaw took another drag, spit out a small piece of tobacco leaf, and held the smoke in until his lungs burned. He looked at the shape of the man's mouth, the way his lips curved inward at an odd angle.

"How long you been doing meth? A while?"

The man's eyes got big, and he started rubbing his hands together faster. He was younger than he looked. Shaw was sure of that now. The drugs had aged and weathered him, but there was still some youth in the way he sat, some strength in his shoulders and arms. He hadn't lived long enough to be completely worn down.

"Listen," Shaw said. "I don't give a shit about what you do. I'm not going to arrest you or lecture you about the meth, alright? You already know that shit will fuck up your life. You know it better than I do. All I care about right now is that body over there."

A sadness entered the man's eyes as he nodded.

"Okay, so you heard something and came out to look. Am I right?"

A nod.

"Did he live here?"

Another sideways shake.

"Sometimes? He came and went?"

A nod.

"Did you know his name?"

A shake.

"So, you come out of your…residence and see No Name over there getting fucked up. Did you see the killer?"

The man's fingers weren't just rubbing together anymore. They were shaking.

"Male, female, tall, short?"

No nod, no shake, but the man's knees started moving, bouncing up and down.

"Listen, I know you saw something. I'm no dummy. You don't sit here staring off into space and rattling like some loose change unless you saw something you didn't want to see. Here's where I'm going to ask you to use your words. You gotta give me something, and I'll tell you why. Because you ain't gonna sleep tonight. You'll be shitting your pants thinking that this person is going to come back for you and take your head because you saw him."

"It's not a person," the man said slowly. His voice was deep and raspy.

Shaw held his breath, afraid to move or speak and break the spell. He had to be patient, let the man find the words. The smoke from Shaw's cigarette curled up and burned his eyes. He saw Robby standing by the cop cars, watching. Shaw put one hand by his side and made a downward motion.

Stay where you are.

"It was standing right over there," the man said, and as he spoke, his hands started moving, scratching his neck, his arms. All the while, his legs kept bouncing.

"Looked like a weird dude at first in a long coat. Had the hood up, so I couldn't really see much. He…it…whatever, it had a real bad limp, you know? Like, dragging his feet and walking like he was so drunk he was gonna fall over."

"And what about him?" Shaw asked, nodding to the corpse.

"Terry," the man said. "His name is Terry. He was fixing one of the tarps and saw this guy, thought maybe he was coming to steal shit. So Terry starts yelling at him to get the fuck out of here."

Shaw took another drag, felt the heat hit his fingers, and dropped it. The orange end hissed out on the wet ground.

"What's your name?"

"Sean."

"Okay, Sean, then what?"

"Then this dude stops. Doesn't say nothing, just stares at Terry for a long time. Terry keeps yelling at him."

The man stopped, looked at Shaw, and says, "Listen, I ain't shot up since yesterday, alright? I'm trying to get my shit together, man. It ain't fucking easy, you know? I just mean I wasn't on anything when I saw it. You don't gotta believe it, but all I can tell you is the truth. Don't got nothing to lose."

Shaw nodded, tried to make his face look sympathetic. Anne always told him that he could sympathize with the scum of the earth—the addicts, the hookers, the thieves, the vandals—but he could never sympathize with normal people. A "flaw in his design," she called it. That statement had messed with his head for weeks because she was right. Maybe it was because the problems on the street felt real, and all the other problems that "normal" people complained about seemed petty and insignificant in comparison. There were no life or death choices, no struggling in the grip of an addiction that stole everything from you, but that you couldn't stop chasing no matter how hard you tried.

"I just want to know what you saw," Shaw said.

Sean took a breath, then lifted his hands and wiggled his fingers as he brought them back down. "The dude in the coat fell apart," he said. "From the top to the bottom, just collapsed."

"He fell down?"

The man shook his head, "No, not like that. Like he wasn't really a person. His coat and everything fell on the ground, then...then this...I don't know what else to call it. This fucking shadow came out of the clothes. This black shadow came spreading out and covered Terry up. I heard him scream a couple of times, but he dropped and got quiet pretty quick. The shadow covered his whole body so that I couldn't even see it. I don't know how much time passed. After a while, the shadow moved back into the clothes, and they filled up, and it looked like a person again. Off it went, limping down the street like nothing. I ran out to check on Terry and—" he nodded toward the body, "—what you see is what I saw."

Shaw had been watching the man the whole time he spoke. The fear was real. That much was clear. Legs bouncing, fingers searching and picking the skin on his hands, his neck. Even the way he breathed while he talked, all signs that he saw something.

Shaw sensed movement near the street corner. He looked past Sean to the edge of the building, squinted into the rain. There it was again, a head poking around the corner of the building, then a hand extended in a wave. Shaw sat up straight, was about to call for Robby when he recognized the shape of the head. The hand waved again, and Shaw waved back.

"Okay," Shaw said. "A person who isn't a person, and a shadow that kills people."

The man snorted, "Jesus, man, were you even listening? Fuck, I don't have to sit here and tell you shit. I'm doing my best. I said I don't know what else to call it. How do you describe something when you have no idea what it is?"

"You're right," Shaw said, "I'm sorry. I just don't know what to do with all of this. What do I even look for?"

The man looked over at the covered body lying in the middle of the street.

"I'm not a fucking detective, but I'd start by looking for a guy in a long coat who walks with a gnarly limp."

3

Shaw had bummed a couple of cigarettes off one of the paramedics who came to take Terry's body to the morgue. He stood under the eaves of the building and smoked as Terry was loaded onto a stretcher and put in the back of the ambulance. They drove away with no lights or sirens because there was nothing urgent in their task. There was no one to save.

Robby got Sean in one of the squad cars and had him taken to the station where he would be questioned further. Shaw wasn't completely convinced that he wasn't out of his mind on something. He didn't seem high, but sometimes they didn't. Sometimes the addicts needed a little something in their system just to seem normal. Maybe a night in jail would sober him up, or maybe his story would stay exactly the same.

Robby came over, stood next to Shaw, and made a big show of waving the cigarette smoke away and coughing dramatically.

"You know my wife thinks I'm the one who's smoking when I come home smelling like shit? I tell her it's you, and she says 'bullshit.' You putting stress on my marriage and killing yourself all at the same time."

Shaw raised his eyebrows, took another drag. "I'm sorry your wife thinks you smell like shit."

Robby put both hands together as in prayer, looked up at the sky. "When I first made detective, I said, 'God, please don't give me an asshole for a partner. That's all I ask.'"

Shaw smiled a little and blew his smoke away from Robby. The rain had slowed to a drizzle, and the sky was now a light gray as morning approached. Shaw's eyes burned from fatigue. He wanted to go home and sleep, but he couldn't stop thinking about what Sean had said.

"Do you believe him?" Robby asked.

"I'm not sure yet," Shaw said. "I think he saw something."

Robby put his hands in his pockets and walked in place to keep warm.

"That was some fucking story. The kind of story someone tells when they're high as balls."

"Maybe."

Robby let out a laugh. "Maybe?"

Shaw pointed at a streetlamp across the street on the corner.

"That light is out. If the man Sean says he saw was standing right over there, it would be hard to see much in front of Terry. Maybe this guy pretended to faint, and when Terry came over to help, he attacked him. Say he's wearing all black, and he's in the shadows. It might look strange."

Robby took his hands out and blew into them.

"Come on. You think that's what happened?"

Shaw dropped the cigarette, ground it out with a heel. "No, I don't."

Robby yawned, looked at his watch. "It's morning, man. You want me to give you a ride home."

Shaw shook his head. "I'll walk."

Robby took out his car keys, twirled them on one finger. "Twenty-two minutes, that's how long it'll take." He tapped his watch. "Time yourself."

Shaw nodded as Robby made his way to the car, then looked over at the homeless encampment and wondered how many people were in there. He couldn't even see a clear entrance to the structure. If he went and tore down the cardboard walls, pushed aside the sleeping bags and tents, he felt pretty sure he'd find at least one person who did not belong there. Someone lost and searching for something that could not be found.

In Shaw's experience, the homeless usually fell into two categories. The first were those who hit a run of bad luck and ended up losing everything. From down that low, it was nearly impossible to climb back up. You needed a job for money, money for food and rent, an address just to get a job. Not to mention a place to shower and get cleaned to interview for the job. Then transportation to get there. The shelters did their best to help people, but Shaw had learned there was a chasm between needing help and admitting that you needed it. So, those people did what they could to survive, sometimes with a spouse and children along.

The second were those who didn't want to live by society's rules, and the only thing they cared about was scraping together enough money for the next high. The street is where they wanted to be. They had tasted and seen, and the real world, with all its corruption and bills and responsibilities and rituals, was nothing compared to the world that appeared on the other side of a needle.

Robby got all worked up about the homeless in the city, wished the mayor would do something about the massive encampments that were popping up and growing all over the place—in the parks, under the overpasses, along the highways, the sidewalks. They'd been called to more than one murder at these camps. And they heard numerous stories about rape from other investigators. The rape bothered Robby more than anything because of his two daughters. Shaw always pointed out that before they were detectives, they'd been called to rapes in some of the nicest houses in the city, too.

o

Shaw stayed on the street long after Robby and the other officers had left. He stood with his back against the brick building and stared at the place in the road where Terry had died. A small crew had come and cleaned up the blood, and there was now a darker patch of asphalt where the body had been. Cleaner. No one driving down this block would ever know a man had been decapitated there.

He waited until the sky brightened a little and walked to the other side of the street. To the place where Sean said he had seen the person in the long coat. Shaw didn't know what he was looking for, but he usually didn't. The things that were out of place had a way of jumping out at him. He once told Anne that certain details seemed to detach from the backdrop and hover before him. Robby called it his "radar," but Shaw always thought of it as instinct. A subconscious awareness of the order of things and recognition of when they had been disrupted.

Even in a place as chaotic as the street, there was a secret order to everything.

Shaw stood against the building where the person in the coat would have been, and he tried to imagine Terry standing in the street, yelling. With that one streetlamp out, the perp would have felt hidden, emboldened maybe.

The motive for the killing would come later, but it was the decapitation that Shaw couldn't stop thinking about. Along with the fact that the head itself was missing.

A trophy. A goddamn trophy is what it was. And Shaw didn't like the echoes of serial killers who kept pieces of their victims stored in fridges, freezers, and bathtubs full of acid. Shrines and altars.

To take a head, though. That was probably the biggest, and therefore hardest removable piece of the human body to hide. You can put a finger in your pocket. A tongue can be hidden inside a fist. But something as big as a head draws attention.

As he thought about it, Shaw put both hands to his own head to judge the size, the weight. He imagined it separated from his neck, leaking blood and fluid, all personality and sense of who he was absolutely drained from the face.

Where does someone go with that kind of trophy? What do they do with it?

He'd seen the murdered and dismembered body of a man, and what bothered him the most was the part he didn't see.

Shaw stood staring at the street until he got dizzy. He reached into his coat for another cigarette, made a mental reminder to buy a pack on the way home, and held a hand to his stomach as it growled. He needed to eat something, get some coffee. His eyes burned even more, but he didn't think he'd be sleeping much when he got home. Calls like this wound his brain up and sent it spinning for days.

With the cigarette clenched between his teeth, Shaw put his hands in his pockets and walked east until he came to the crosswalk. He turned right and walked until the cigarette burned down to the filter. He came to a small coffee shop. A bell above the door rang as he opened the door and stepped inside. He ordered two black coffees, one "everything" bagel, and one plain wheat bagel. He didn't care for wheat, but he figured it had to be healthier than the others.

He paid in cash and left with a bag and small tray for the coffees.

Shaw walked back the way he'd come. Back toward the homeless encampment. Cars drove by now, people emerged from apartment buildings and walked to coffee shops, jobs. Out of one building and into another.

Anne used to tell him that part of the reason he became a cop, then a detective, was because he could never stay in one place for long. She was probably right about that if he was honest. The calls were often tragic, sometimes heartbreaking, but he was in a different place all the time. Chasing leads, tips. Interviewing suspects, witnesses. Anne had also said the same was true about his relationships.

ALONG THE SHADOW

His restless personality led him to disconnect and seek out something, someone new.

Shaw didn't believe her about that. If anything, it was Anne projecting her fear onto him. Which was ironic because she was the one who left him. She molded some version of her husband, crafted out of fear and insecurity, shot it through with the lightning of her anger, and inadvertently created in him the person she feared was already there.

He walked past entire blocks that looked like something from a movie about the future where the gap between the rich and the poor becomes a chasm that can't be bridged. Too many tents and encampments to count. Some may have started as separate structures, but they eventually grew together, expanded, and took over. Entire blocks where he couldn't even stay on the sidewalk. He passed a few homeless people, either up early or still wandering in the haze of whatever substance they'd done the night before. Or…those who weren't high at the moment but had done so many drugs that their state of existence was permanently altered, their brain rewired to see things that weren't really there.

He crossed the street at Everett, took a glance at

the place where Terry's body had been found, and kept going. Up ahead, he saw a man sitting on the steps of an old building. Graffiti was sprayed on the bricks. Symbols and strange words that only meant anything to the one who painted them.

"Hey, Manny," Shaw said, sitting down next to him.

The man stood quickly and bowed. "I've been waiting for you."

"I know," Shaw said. "Sit."

Manny sat down, his dark jeans and coat streaked with stains. The smell of body odor was so strong Shaw considered lighting a cigarette just to cover it up. He gave Manny one of the coffees, took out the "everything" bagel, and handed it over.

"Many thanks, kind sir," Manny said and took a bite. He closed his eyes and chewed, his lips curled in a smile as if the bagel were a delicacy. Shaw noted the thin, white scar and asymmetry of a repaired cleft lip.

"Crazy night, eh?" Manny said, mouth still of bagel.

"How long I known you, Manny?"

Manny closed his eyes again. This time scrunched tight.

"Three years, four months, and...almost two weeks," he said. "In three days, it will be two weeks."

Shaw nodded. That sounded right, and it probably was. Manuel Rodriguez was one of those rare homeless who preferred to be by himself. He had no need for others, and he somehow managed to stay relatively healthy. Shaw had taken him to the hospital only once, and he was treated for dehydration then released.

"In that time," Shaw said, "do you think the world has gotten better or worse?"

Manny laughed, and some half-chewed bagel fell out of his mouth.

"From where I sit, it all looks the same to me."

That was probably right, too. Get down low enough, and everything is above you. Nothing changes that far down.

Manny stopped chewing and held the bagel up in front of him, squinted at it. His mouth moved silently.

"Manny," Shaw said, "Stop counting the seeds. Just eat."

Shaw took one bite of his bagel, swallowed it, and wished he had ordered something different. He put it back in the bag, lit a cigarette, and took a drink of coffee.

"Tell me what you saw last night."

Manny held what was left of the bagel in two hands, almost delicately, and took a small bite.

"I heard what the tweaker told you," he said. "Tweaker or no, he's not wrong about the guy in the long coat. The guy who walks with a limp. It's more than a limp, though, boss. It's his whole body."

He set the bagel down, stood, and demonstrated by walking on the sidewalk in front of Shaw.

"He leans really far with each step, like this. Drags one foot, then the other." He stopped, looked up to the sky for a moment, then said, "It's like he's not used to walking. Or, the body in the coat is really fucked up."

Manny sat back down and picked up his bagel. "Why didn't you get cream cheese? You always gotta eat a bagel with cream cheese, man."

Shaw patted his stomach. "Empty calories."

Manny burst out laughing, giving Shaw a clear view of the chewed-up bagel in his mouth.

"Empty calories? Shit, man, that ain't no way to live."

Back when they'd first met, Manny had told Shaw the story of how he had come to be on the street, and the plot points were common to many Shaw had met over the years. In Manny's case, he was the sole provider for his wife and three kids. Two things happened at once that completely overturned his life. First, he lost his job as a car salesman, and then his wife admitted to having an affair with a wealthy man she'd met at the gym. She divorced Manny, got sole custody of the kids, and Manny was very suddenly without a home, a job, or a family. In his depression, he took what little cash he had and used it to score some heroin. That first stab of the needle flipped a switch in his brain, and he decided he would chase that feeling until he couldn't any longer. Which made Manny a strange sort of addict, but the kind Shaw saw a lot these days—the addict who isn't frequently high but spends most days trying to scrounge together enough money to get a hit. Which meant he was only high, maybe once a week.

"Have you ever seen this guy before?" Shaw asked.

Mouth still full, Manny shook his head.

"You think if I throw you a few bucks, you could ask around, see if anyone else has seen him?"

With the bagel gone, Manny moved on to the coffee. He took one sip, made a face, and looked at Shaw. "No cream or sugar either? Shit."

When Shaw met Manny, a question came into his mind that was truer now than it was back then.

What is the difference between us? What stops me from being where he is?

It wasn't bottom until you couldn't fall any further. And once you hit that place, what motivated some to try and claw their way back up while others just stayed where they fell?

"Yeah, sure," Manny said, taking another drink and grimacing. "Hundred bucks sound fair?"

Shaw took out his wallet, only had a twenty and a couple of ones.

"Let's head to my place. I'll get you cash."

Manny smiled, and Shaw had forgotten that the homeless man's smile had some gaps in it. Missing teeth that marked the years, the life he had spent on the streets. Eventually, the rest would be gone too.

"It's only a matter of time," Shaw said out loud, without thinking.

Manny gave him a confused look.

"Shit, man, everything is a matter of time."

4

In another time, another life, Shaw might have been worried about bringing a homeless man to his apartment. But these days, he didn't care. Didn't care who saw him, what they thought, or even if Manny decided to steal something, which Shaw didn't think he'd do. They climbed the stairs to the third floor. Shaw unlocked the door and led Manny in.

"This your place, uh?" Manny said, taking a slow walk around the living room and looking at Shaw's meager possessions. He smiled at the telescope, mumbled something about how he used to have one when he was a kid. Manny stopped at a framed picture of Anne and the kids. Shaw had thought about cutting her out, but it would be vindictive, and he didn't want the boys thinking he was bitter.

"I thought you'd live somewhere nicer," Manny said. "That cop salary ain't much, is it?"

"Detective," Shaw said. "And no, it's not much when you have to pay alimony and child support."

"Never had that problem," Manny said and smiled big, but the smile fell apart, faded, almost immediately.

Shaw dug through a drawer in the kitchen, took out a roll of cash secured with a frayed rubber band. He pulled five twenties from it and put the roll back. He also took out an old cell phone, a flip model that used to be for his oldest boy, until Anne got him a smartphone. Something Shaw thought was the dumbest idea in the world. The flip phone was still activated and on his plan for another month.

Manny stood near the window that looked down over the street and watched the people walking by.

"It's weird being able to so many people all at once," he said quietly. He held up his hand, thumb, and forefinger an inch apart. "They're so small, but each one of them has a whole life."

"Sometimes, I think the same thing," Shaw told him. "I do that whenever I'm called to a crime scene. I have to remind myself that the dead thing I'm looking at might have been one of those people walking under my window. Dreams, job, kids, husband, wife…you know. Fighting depression, hopelessness. Just a person."

Shaw turned the phone on and handed it and the money over to Manny.

"Hundred bucks, and the phone to call if you see or hear anything. Call anytime, no matter how late, alright? Time matters."

"You're fucking right, it does," Manny said, staring at the money. "I'll find you something."

Shaw walked him to the door, and Manny stopped, held up the cash.

"Listen, you know where this is going, right?"

"It's your money," Shaw said. "You do what you feel you need to."

Manny bit his lip, nodded, and started down the stairs.

"I'm gonna find you that limping man," he called out. "Bet I can run faster than him."

Manny's laughter echoed down the stairs until Shaw closed the door. He stood in silence, thoughts tumbling through his head. He went over to the couch and laid down. No wife, no kids.

    So quiet it hurt.

5

Shaw woke up in a dark room to the sound of buzzing. He sat up fast, unsure where he was at first. His cell phone vibrated on the coffee table with a noise like something coming apart. Outside the window, it was night, and all he could see were the lights from windows in the building across the street.

He grabbed the phone.

"Shaw," he said with a hoarse voice.

"Since we're partners and all, I think it's common courtesy to let me know where you go when you leave a crime scene," Robby said.

Shaw pulled the phone away from his ear and looked at the time. He had slept all day and into the night.

It was after 10 p.m. He made his way to the bathroom, flipping on lights as he went.

"I didn't mean to fall asleep," Shaw said. "Any luck with Sean?"

"Who?"

"Pendejo," Shaw said. "Did he say anything else?"

"He knew enough to ask for a lawyer, but I don't think he knew any more than what he told you, which needs to be written down. Did you take notes or anything?"

Shaw unzipped his fly and pissed into the toilet. "No."

"Shit, man," Robby said. "Are you taking a leak while talking to me?"

"Rinsing off dishes," Shaw said.

"I know the sound of piss of when I hear it. You can't fool me. Listen, hermano, you gotta write this shit down, fill out the paperwork, you know? You left me holding my dick, and I know that's what you're doing right now, but you gotta help me out."

Shaw thought about flushing, but he didn't want to hear Robby say, "I knew it," so he let it be, went to the kitchen, and took a beer out of the fridge.

"You remember Manny?" Shaw asked.

ALONG THE SHADOW

"Your hobo friend?"

"Yeah. He saw the guy in the hooded coat."

"No shit?"

"No shit. Described him the same way Sean did. I gave Manny an old cell phone and a hundred bucks. He's going to keep an eye out for me."

Robby sighed loud, and it came through the earpiece as static.

"You gave a hundred bucks to a homeless guy? And a phone? Dios mio, puta. That fucker is off in outer space, right, and you're sitting around waiting for a phone call?"

"Nah, Manny's alright," Shaw said. "Guy's just looking for some purpose, and now he has it. Should've seen his face. He's a private eye now, Robby."

Robby sighed again. "You seriously think he's going to look for him?"

"I hope so," Shaw said.

"Yeah, yeah. Hope in one hand, shit in the other. See which one fills up faster."

A noise came through, a steady pulsing beep. Shaw pulled the phone away and saw another call on the screen.

"Speak of the devil," Shaw said. "He's calling now."

"Probably fucking high. Call me after."

Shaw hung up on Robby and picked up the other call. At first, all he heard was background noise. Voices, shouting, music, laughter.

"Shaw? Shaw, can you hear me?"

Manny's voice, yelling above the noise.

"Where are you?" Shaw said, yelling back.

"I found him."

Shaw's hand gripped the bottle of beer tighter.

"Manny, where are you?"

"I'm by the Timbers Stadium. A game just ended, and everyone is leaving."

The soccer stadium where the Portland Timbers played their home games wasn't far, and Shaw could be there in fifteen minutes if he hurried. Manny's breath came huffing through the phone.

"I thought maybe he was coming here to set up, you know, ask for money. But the dude is just staying outside the crowd. Away from the lights, it looks like. I don't know, but he's shuffling around."

"Did he see you?"

"Nah, man. I'm stealthy. Keeping my distance."

"Stay on him," Shaw said, dumping the beer down the kitchen sink and grabbing his keys off the counter.

ALONG THE SHADOW

"Don't let him out of your sight. I'm on my way."

Shaw snatched his gun and badge from the coffee table and put on his coat as he walked out the door. As soon as he hit the street, he started running toward the Stadium. After a game, the Pearl District was flooded with spectators packing into bars and restaurants. Every sidewalk would be filled with drunk soccer fans waving their team scarves, getting into fights, and looking for places to drink more. The crowd would be good for staying hidden, but it would also make it harder to follow someone.

Shaw ran until he came to Burnside—the main street that ran east to west through the city. He took a right and kept running. As he crossed the 405 overpass, he ran past groups of people dressed in the green and yellow sweatshirts and hats of the Timbers. Just on the other side of the overpass, the sidewalks were already full. Up ahead, he saw a bright halo of light above the stadium.

He shouldered through a group of twentysomething-year-olds laughing, shoving, taking selfies until he came to the front of the stadium and found himself standing in front of a giant, hollowed-out, laughing face. Shaw came to a dead stop, heart hammering, blood rushing through his ears. It had been so long since he came this way, he had forgotten about the sculptures. Two of them, nearly eight feet tall and made of what looked like bands of bronze fashioned into a grinning mask, stationed at either side of the stadium.

Shaw took out his phone and hit callback.

Manny answered but didn't say anything. Neither did Shaw. He heard footsteps, breathing, voices in the background.

Finally, "I've still got him. He's moving away from the crowd. Not very fast. He's not talking to anyone. One guy tried to hand him some money, but the dude didn't take it, and the cash just fell on the ground, and he kept on going."

"Where is he?"

"I don't, man. Morrison, I think. Hold up…he's stopping. Now he just went between some buildings."

"Okay, Manny, hang tight. Just wait there for me."

"What is he doing?"

Shaw took off running again, going around the empty eyes and mouth of the sculpture, and headed towards 18th.

"Manny, did you hear what I said?"

"I think he's going to break in or something,"

Manny's whispered voice said.

"Stay where you are."

There was a crash through the speaker. The sound of a trash can falling over, spilling its contents all the ground.

Shaw saw the sign for Morrison and tore down the street, his lungs burning. It was a side street with no places to eat or drink, so it was dark and empty except for some cars parked along the curb. Old buildings that housed mechanics, businesses.

"Manny, you staying put?" Shaw said.

A rustle of movement, as if the phone were against Manny's leg.

Manny's voice, muffled. "Hey. What the fuck are you doing?"

Silence. Breathing.

"Holy shit."

A high-pitched screech, more movement. Manny saying "Oh shit, oh shit," over and over.

Then a crack as the phone fell, Manny's voice yelling "Get off me!" and then another sound that Shaw thought at first was static. A rapid chattering that reminded him of a playing card clipped to the spokes of a bike tire spinning a hundred miles an hour.

Something hit the phone, and it scraped along the ground.

Shaw took off running, yelling Manny's name into the phone. All he heard were grunts and groans now.

"No, no, no."

Then a scream pierced the quiet street, full of fear and pain. Shaw heard it coming from up the block only a fraction of a second before it came through the phone he still held to his ear. The scream became a gurgle, the sound of thick liquid gathering in the back of a throat.

Shaw let the hand holding the phone fall to his side so he could run faster. With his other hand, he reached back to his waist and unholstered the gun.

He saw a break between two buildings up ahead, an alley. He came to a stop and tried to catch his breath. He slipped the phone into his back pocket and gripped the gun tight with both hands. He steadied his shaking muscles, breathed deep, and quickly swung into the alley, gun pointed straight ahead. A single weak light shone down on the garbage cans and dumpster, the wooden pallets, and black trash bags.

Lying on the ground about halfway down was a

body. Shaw was staring at the soles of the shoes.

"Manny?" he said quietly. No response, no movement.

A small light glowed several feet away from the body. The still open cell phone.

As his eyes adjusted, Shaw saw several small, circular lights wink on and off from various points in the alley. He blinked hard, looked again. Ten or more appeared under one of the dumpsters, then vanished as he took a few steps forward. More came from further down, hidden in shadow, and they made him think of the stars he saw through his telescope. He held up a hand over his eyes, squinted, and they were gone. He heard small rustling movements, crinkling the trash bags, rippling the water in a puddle.

"I'm a cop," Shaw said, trying to make his voice sound strong and not out of breath. "I can see you, and I have a gun trained right at your head. Step out with both hands high, and I won't shoot."

More of those small lights came and went, and Shaw wondered if maybe his dizziness and blurry vision after running were causing him to see things that weren't really there. He tightened his sweaty grip on the gun and ran forward, past the body lying face down and toward the back of the alley. His finger was ready to squeeze the trigger the moment someone stepped out of the shadows.

The alley ended in a brick wall—trash piled high against it. Scurrying sounds came from all around, moving along the shadow and rushing past him. This far down, he could see into the corners of the alley. There was nothing, no one. Just a few torn open trash bags spilling out old clothes, shoes.

Keeping his gun at the ready, Shaw said Manny's name one more time, turned around and saw why he hadn't responded. The man's head was gone.

6

Days went by. Shaw's two boys came to stay with him for the weekend, and he tried his best to be "on" for them, but every time one of them mentioned how much better things were at home, it was a little dagger in Shaw's heart. The oldest had a TV in his room now. Something Shaw would never have allowed. The youngest was able to play video games every day. Something else Shaw would not have been okay with. As it was now, he didn't have any video game consoles, and the TV was not only old, it didn't have cable. He had to put up with the whining and pouting and only barely managed to avoid losing his temper by ordering pizza, something their health-conscious mother frowned upon. The oldest rolled his eyes and sighed when

Shaw told him he'd be sleeping on the couch. The youngest was okay with sleeping in Shaw's bed, but it was only another reminder that this small, one-bedroom apartment was more like a cheap hotel than a home.

Shaw lay awake in bed with his son asleep beside him, and the boy's breathing patterns, the way he shifted, rolled, and wrapped himself in the blankets, kept Shaw from fully relaxing. He stared at the ceiling and replayed the night he found Manny's body. He even dreamed it some nights. Not a fantasy or a nightmare, but a dream in which everything happened exactly as it had in real life.

In these dreams, Shaw was able to slow down and focus on the details he could not fully see that night. He discovered that he was able to manipulate time, slow it down. He moved past Manny's body, barely registering that the head was missing, and blood was still squirting from the severed artery in his neck. He stood and stared into the darkness of the alley, feeling certain the killer was present somewhere. Hiding. And it drove him crazy that he couldn't see him, find him. The sense of being looked at, observed was so strong that it made the hairs on his arms stand up. Made a chill run down his back. Did the dark move? Did the shadows slowly crawl along the edge of the buildings like ink in water? It looked like it. Even more importantly, it felt like it, and Shaw had learned to trust those feelings over the years, no matter how crazy they seemed.

He got out of bed, went into the living room, and listened to the sound of his oldest son's breathing. Eyes closed, mouth open, and body draped on the couch.

To sleep so deeply, Shaw thought. *When does that end? When do we will our ability to find that much peace?*

He went over to the telescope, thought about opening the window for a clearer view, but decided not to risk waking his son. He closed one eye and put the other to the eyepiece. He didn't expect to see much because of all the clouds, but he liked knowing the stars were out there, even if they were hidden. He knew they were burning in the dark, bright and constant. He had to believe the future was out there as well. Clear and beautiful, hidden behind the smoke of all the fires he'd started. Someday he would see it once all the smoke cleared.

The following morning, over a breakfast of sugar cereal and toaster pastries (another "not allowed" by Anne), the youngest let it slip that mom had a new special friend who sometimes stayed the night, and a dam broke in Shaw's head, spilling dark thoughts all over his brain. He told the boys to finish their breakfast, and he left the apartment, went downstairs, stood outside on the sidewalk, and chain-smoked two cigarettes. He ignored the oldest telling him how bad he smelled when he came back in. Shaw went into the bathroom, brushed his teeth, and stared at himself in the mirror. He didn't hate what he saw, but he didn't like it either.

He looked lost.

o

Shaw had never been one to carry guilt that was not his or one to blame himself for the actions of others. During his years as a detective, he had to let go of the inclination to own the death and tragedy he witnessed. He could not prevent someone out there from committing random acts of violence, no matter how carefully he analyzed a crime scene or interviewed witnesses. In a city of over half a million people, it was impossible to stop a murder from happening. The best he could hope for is that he'd be able to find and arrest the one responsible. The loss, however, was already over and done with. The blood spilled, the lives stolen. No turning back the clocks on those deaths.

A few hours after Anne had come and picked up the boys—she waited in the car and did not make eye contact while Shaw carried their bags downstairs and hugged them both—Shaw stood at the window looking down at the street, and he felt a sudden surge of guilt over Manny. It was irrational, but it came on with such force that Shaw had trouble breathing.

A life, gone. All because Shaw gave him a cell phone and asked him to keep an eye out. He couldn't have known where that request would lead. Manny didn't carry any I.D., and there was no way to contact family members, so his headless body remained in a chilled drawer in the county morgue as evidence. An autopsy would be performed at some point, and Shaw would have to read it, imagine it, and hear it all over again. Shaw wasn't even sure Rodriguez was Manny's last name. He thought he'd heard him say it once but never asked again.

Shaw would not allow himself to think *this is my fault* because it wasn't. It was the fault of the murderer, and if Shaw started blaming himself instead of the one responsible, it would only impair his ability to be objective.

Still, what he felt was dangerously close to being at fault, and that feeling made him sick to his stomach.

Robby had called several times since Manny's death, but Shaw let the calls go to voicemail. He didn't want to talk about it or think about it. There was something he couldn't see in these deaths, something at the edges, in the shadows.

The walls of the apartment seemed to shift, to inch forward ever so slowly. He needed to get out. He needed open air. He would walk and smoke and think of something other than headless corpses bleeding out on Portland streets. What that was, he didn't yet know, but he had learned it was best to be in motion. Always in motion. Anne would have called it "running away from his emotions," but he knew better. Sometimes running from one thing is just chasing down something else.

He grabbed his keys and cigarettes. The badge and gun sat on the coffee table, and he thought about taking them, then decided against it. He didn't want to be a detective tonight.

7

Shaw made his way downtown on Burnside. A concert was just letting out at the Roseland Theater, and the sidewalks were filled with people, mostly young, still buzzing on the high of live music played loud. He smiled a little. He remembered coming to see bands here when he was young. Back when all the problems he had seemed so small compared to the problems that would be waiting for him in the future. He had even brought Anne to the Roseland on one of their first dates to see the band Film Score. An indie band with moderate success. None of these kids would have heard of them, but they were good, and Shaw loved them then. He and Anne had their first kiss that night after the show. His ears were still ringing, and his heart was pounding like a bass drum when she leaned in and pressed her soft lips against his. Love. It felt like it could never end.

He knew better now. Love wasn't magical, not even close. It was like a fire, and it did not burn indefinitely. It had to be fed, tended, cared for. If you turned away, it could torch everything around you, or worse, burn out and die.

What a shame, he thought, *that the most important lessons in life are learned through failure.*

Thinking of that date made him miss Anne. They had something good until it wasn't anymore, and the heaviest part of the weight was on him. He had failed her. He'd believed love would always be there. He took her for granted, and he knew that now. Now that the papers were signed and she had moved on.

As Shaw walked into Old Town Chinatown, he thought about calling Anne, apologizing for all his faults and flaws. Maybe just saying the words out loud would change something in him. He didn't expect her to take him back, but maybe acknowledging his failures could help heal her heart. All that anger had to be pain, right?

He turned left, walked through the traditional

ALONG THE SHADOW

Chinese archway guarded by two lion statues. Another part of the city that used to be so unique was now just another dark and uninviting section where crime, drugs, and murder hid. Half the streetlamps were burned out, and he walked several blocks in the dark. The streets were empty, quiet. If he wanted, he could walk west to Everett, where Terry's body had been found. He was sure Sean was back in the encampment, probably out of his mind on whatever he'd been able to score.

No. He didn't want to be back there. He'd keep walking until he couldn't walk anymore, then he'd head home.

Finally, he made it to a block with a working street lamp, and it cast a weak yellow circle on the ground. It flickered and dimmed with a harsh buzzing sound as he walked under it. He passed an alleyway on the left. Dark, filled with trash and rainwater. He kept going, hands deep in his pockets, fingers rubbing his pack of cigarettes. He hadn't lit one yet. Told himself he didn't need it. It was one of a thousand things that bothered Anne. If he could make it back home without lighting up, maybe that would mean something.

He crossed the street and moved to another block,

this one dark. Another alleyway. Shaw decided he didn't want to be out any more. He wanted to be back at home. Maybe he'd call Anne, leave a message if she didn't pick up. He'd leave a message for the kids too. Tell them he was sorry for being grouchy. He'd call Robby, too, apologize for being an asshole. Selfish, that's what he'd been. So many things to make right. It made his head hurt.

Shaw didn't mean to look as he passed the alley. Didn't mean to turn his head and peer into the dark, narrow space. But he did, and his heart tripped over two beats, paused, then came back with a heaviness that made it hard to breathe.

A figure stood halfway down. It wore a long coat, and the hood was pulled up over its head. The streetlamp flickered on for a moment, and in the quick burst of light, there was something familiar about the figure.

Shaw took one step into the alley, and his foot splashed in a puddle. The streetlamp buzzed and went out. The figure's head moved slowly from side to side. Shaw squinted into the dark. There was definitely something familiar about him.

Another flicker and Shaw saw the cleft lip.

"Manny?"

ALONG THE SHADOW

At the sound of his voice, the figure went into motion. The legs jerked forward, dragging each foot as it rushed closer. The arms lifted, spread out wide, and that was when Shaw noticed the shadows in the alleyway shifting, gathering, flowing toward him like dark liquid. And there was a sound too, the same sound he had heard on the phone when Manny was killed.

The light flickered again, and the face in the hood was clear for just a moment. Manny's face, he was sure of it now. The mouth was partially open, revealing a black tongue, and the eyes were glossy gray. Lifeless.

The light flickered out, and the shadows crept along the ground, forming a wave of darkness that crashed into his legs, surrounded him as the figure stumbled so close Shaw could smell rancid meat. That chattering, scratching sound was so loud now, it was all Shaw could hear. The figure loomed over him. Then, all at once, it lost shape. The jacket and pants went limp, hung in the air momentarily, and fluttered to the ground. Something rolled out of the hood, but before Shaw had a chance to see what it was, the shadows had gathered all around him and moved up his legs, covered his stomach and chest. The shadows were sharp. They had teeth and claws that tore into his flesh.

Shaw screamed as he felt warm blood pouring down his body. He turned to run, and the shadows sliced through the tendon in his right ankle. An electric pain shot up his leg just before it went numb. He lost his balance and fell to the ground. The shadows were warm as they covered him. The weight of them pressed down on his chest. The sound was so loud now, filling his ears. He kept thinking, *this is not the future I saw through the telescope. This is not the future I saw.* His vision narrowed, began to dim, and the last thing he saw was the severed head of Manuel Rodriguez staring at him with dead eyes as rats crawled all over his face.

8

A figure in an oversized coat, hood pulled up over its head, stumbled out of the alleyway just as thunder cracked and rain began falling from the sky. The upper body tilted forward as the right foot moved, then the left dragging behind it. It continued in this way down the empty street. It avoided light when it could, stayed close to the buildings, occasionally scraping its shoulder against the brick as it swayed.

The figure moved west up another street, walking as though its body had been shattered then reassembled. Each step was crooked, twisted, and each arm flailed with the motion.

Rain soaked the long coat, ran down the pants into

the worn-out shoes.

A light shone up ahead and illuminated a glass door. Someone else was coming down the street, and the figure stopped, waited.

A woman, carrying an umbrella in one hand and a grocery bag in the other, approached the glass door. She carefully folded the umbrella, pushed open the door, and went into the building.

The figure waited, shivered, then started walking again. It neared the door and slowly lifted one shaking arm to push it open. The woman stood just inside, and she turned at the sound. The figure shivered again, then walked into the lobby of the Parkrose Apartments.

THANKS

To The Lie Factory—Dan, Nicole, Scott,
Sunshine, Tricia, Michele, Bennett, Justin, Jeremy—
this one's got teeth.

And to Chuck Palahniuk, for everything.

ABOUT THE AUTHOR

Tyler Jones is the author of *Criterium*, *The Dark Side of the Room*, *Enter Softly*, and *Almost Ruth*. His work has appeared in the anthologies *Midnight from Beyond the Stars*, *Flame Tree Press: Chilling Crime Short Stories*, *Campfire Macabre*, *Paranormal Contact*, *Burnt Tongues*, *One Thing Was Certain*, *101 Proof Horror*, and in *Dark Moon Digest*, *Coffin Bell*, *Cemetery Dance*, *LitReactor*, *Aphotic Realm*, and *The NoSleep Podcast*.

His stories have been optioned for film.

He lives in Portland, Oregon.

www.tylerjones.net
Twitter: @tjoneswriter
Instagram: @tjoneswriter

TYLER JONES

CRITERIUM
Extended Edition

Includes an introduction by Jeremy Robert Johnson (*The Loop*) and the novella *Enter Softly*

Available in paperback, hardcover, audiobook, and ebook

"This is small-town Bradbury with a world-weary mean streak: even the magic here seems perfectly happy to break your bones and drag your face across asphalt."
**—Jeremy Robert Johnson,
    author of *The Loop* and *Entropy in Bloom***

"Haunting, uncanny and profound: the strongest and most compelling new voice that I've read in a very long time."
**—Michael Marshall Smith,
    author of *Only Forward* and *The Straw Men***

"*Criterium* is a haunting, visceral, gripping story filled with symbolism and allegory. Buckle up for a wild ride that will leave you bruised, shaken, and filled with dread. Tyler Jones is an author to keep an eye on."
**—Richard Thomas, author of *Disintegration*
    and *Spontaneous Human Combustion***

ALMOST RUTH

TYLER JONES

ALMOST RUTH

Available in paperback, hardcover, and ebook

Ashville is a town with a secret history. Ancient structures lie hidden in the woods, and strange rituals are performed to keep the dead where they belong. For gravedigger Abel Cunningham, it is also a town filled with regrets. And when Abel is tasked with an unusual burial, he discovers there are more than just corpses in the cemetery.

Set in an unsettling vision of the Old West, **Almost Ruth** is the new nightmare from the author of **Criterium** and **The Dark Side of the Room**

"Tyler Jones writes with the lyrical complexity and haunting tenderness of masters like Matheson and Straub while remaining entirely new and inventive. A true visionary of contemporary horror fiction."
—**Eric LaRocca, author of** *Things Have Gotten Worse Since We Last Spoke*

"Tyler Jones shows us in *Almost Ruth* that he is a fierce talent in the horror genre and one not to be missed, with prose as sharp as a scalpel he cuts us wide open and pours salt into our wounds."
—**Ross Jeffery, Bram Stoker Nominated author of** *Tome, Juniper,* **and** *Only The Stains Remain*

"With unmatched depth and painstaking beauty, Jones crafts a story focused on small town rituals reminiscent of Shirley Jackson. One that will keep your gears turning and your blood chilled long after the last page."
—**Brennan LaFaro, author of** *Slattery Falls*

TYLER JONES

ENTER SOFTLY

ENTER SOFTLY

Available in paperback, hardcover, and ebook

Enter Softly collects the brand new novellas that are included in the extended editions of ***Criterium***, ***The Dark Side of the Room***, and the new novel ***Almost Ruth***.

In ***Along the Shadow***, a story from the world of ***The Dark Side of the Room***, Detective Gary Shaw is called to the scene of an unusual and grisly murder, which leads him to chase after a strange suspect. But Shaw is not sure if the suspect is also chasing him'.

The butler for a wealthy family begins to fear the worst when mysterious guests show up at the manor in ***Wake Up***, a prequel story to the novel ***Almost Ruth***.

And in ***Enter Softly***, Emergency Room nurse, Lisa Morton, has a problem and she is about to lose her marriage, her child, and her job. As she works the night shift a very damaged patient comes into the hospital and sets in motion a series of events that could lead to Lisa's salvation, or her end. A companion novella to the critically acclaimed ***Criterium***, Tyler Jones returns to a world where addiction is a force with teeth and claws, and it will not let you go quietly.

BURN THE PLANS

coming 2022 from Cemetery Gates Media

From Tyler Jones (author of *Criterium*, *The Dark Side of the Room*, and *Almost Ruth*) comes *Burn the Plans*, a collection featuring fourteen tales of supernatural suspense.

In "A Sharp Black Line", children go missing whenever a ghostly island appears in the center of a river during a storm, and a father must make a terrible choice.

Two young brothers are tasked with burying the family dog, and uncover dark family secrets in "Trigger."

In "Red Hands", a disturbed man goes on a killing spree, and his childhood friend suspects it has something to do with what they found, many years ago, hidden in a cave.

A courtroom sketch artist draws the evil she cannot see in "The Devil on the Stand."

A young boy sets out to get photographic proof of the ghosts that haunt his home in "Boo!"

Grotesque government experiments, a remote viewer who blurs past and future, a crate that contains ancient evil, and bloodthirsty machines are all part of the world in which these tales take place.

Featuring thirteen short stories and one novelette, Burn the Plans is a relentless journey into the dark places we end up when all of our plans go wrong.

Printed in Great Britain
by Amazon